Sugar And Spice And Not So Nice

This is a work of fiction. Names, characters, places, and incidents either are the product of the author's imagination or are used fictitiously, and any resemblance to actual persons, living or dead, business establishments, events, or location is entirely coincidental. The publisher does not have any control over and does not assume any responsibility for author or third-party websites or their content.

Sugar And Spice And Not So Nice

Copyright © 2012 Janet McNulty
Cover Illustration by Robert M. Henry
Cover Design by Robert M. Henry
Interior Text Design by Janet McNulty

ISBN-13: 978-1-941488-95-9
ISBN-10: 1-941488-95-1

For any who have ever met a ghost.

Sugar And Spice And Not So Nice

Janet McNulty

Chapter 1

My name is Mellow Summers and I am twenty-six years old. I was never one to believe in ghosts, but all that changed the day I decided to attend a university up in Vermont. I don't know why I wanted to go to Vermont, considering that I hate the cold. I guess I just wanted to get away from my parents for a while, who had made it their mission in life to tell me how to live. Anyway, like I said, I never believed in ghosts. That is, not until I met Rachel.

It was a beautiful September day when I drove into the apartment complex where I had recently signed a lease. I had no desire to live in the dorms with a bunch of teenagers who had just left home, and were busy living it up at the bars. With my own place, I figured I'd be able to study and have my peace and quiet.

I parked my clunker in the first available space in the parking lot.

"Hey, Mel," yelled my friend Jackie as she ran up to me while I heaved my suitcase out of the backseat. Jackie decided to come to Vermont with me. She wasn't attending classes, but insisted that she needed a change in scenery. I was happy to have a friend with me and an extra person to help with the rent.

"Mel," Jackie said, "you made it. Mr. Carver is waiting for us upstairs."

I followed Jackie up the stairs to the second floor where our apartment was. It was a simple two bedroom, two bathroom flat. I wasn't about to complain since we were only paying $600 a month and it was already furnished.

"Ladies," Mr. Carver greeted us at the door.

I dropped my suitcase, panting from the climb. I really needed some exercise.

"Mr. Carver," I said, "did we forget to sign something?"

"No," he replied. "I just wanted to make certain that you two got settled and to give you these keys." He plopped the keys in my outstretched hand.

"Hey, Mr. Carver, doesn't the average rent for a place like this run a few hundred higher?" asked Jackie.

"Are you complaining about the rent?"

"No," replied Jackie, "I just wondered why you are so willing to rent this to us so cheap."

Mr. Carver sighed heavily. I could have smacked Jackie for this. Why ask such a question when you get a great deal? "The former tenant who lived here was murdered," said Mr. Carver. "Some believe that her spirit haunts this place. By the way, your lease is for one year and there will be no deposit refund if you choose to break it."

"Geez, grouchy isn't he," said Jackie as Mr. Carver left.

"Did you have to ask him about the rent?" I asked.

"I was just curious," said Jackie as we hauled our stuff inside.

The apartment was beautifully furnished. The entrance led us straight into the living room, which was filled with two fluffy couches and an entertainment set. To the right lay the kitchen, complete with dishes and pots and pans. To the left was the hallway, taking you straight to the bedrooms and bathrooms.

"I don't care if this place is haunted," said Jackie as she plopped down on the couch. "You couldn't pay me to leave this place."

Admiring the décor of the apartment, I shared Jackie's sentiment. This was a nice place, and affordable. What more could a college kid want?

"Drop your stuff," said Jackie jumping to her feet. "Let's go for a drive around town and see what the locals are up to."

I didn't argue with her. Going for a drive seemed like a perfect idea for such a beautiful, sunny day. We moseyed along downtown, eyeing all of the small shops and cafes. Jackie became more excited with each new shop she found. She loved shopping. As for me, I only shopped when necessary.

We had been friends since we were in high school. Jackie was always the picture perfect model and very outgoing. With her long black hair and Asian features, she was gorgeous and she knew how to dress it up.

Compare that to my shyness and typical outfit of jeans and a t-shirt. As for doing my hair, I usually threw it in a ponytail and called it good. But we became fast friends. Jackie always had my back. Her spunkiness helped me get rid of a few unfavorable boyfriends and some of it rubbed off on me. I was overjoyed when she agreed to come with me to Vermont.

"Oh, look at that shop," exclaimed Jackie. She pulled into a parking space and we hopped out of the car. We strolled into the store. Jackie immediately grabbed a teal green jacket off of a rack and held it up to me.

"What are you doing?" I asked.

"Seeing if this fits you," she replied. "The color matches your eyes perfectly. And it's only twenty dollars. Now we need a new blouse and slacks to match. And don't forget the shoes."

"Jackie, I don't have the money for this."

"Don't worry about it. I got it."

"Where did you get the money?"

"I have my secrets."

Reluctantly, I allowed Jackie to pull me from rack to rack. She found a purple blouse that complimented the jacket. Before we were done, Jackie managed to fit me into a pair of black slacks and ballet flats. Seventy dollars later I had a complete outfit to start off the new semester. I had to hand it to Jackie. The girl knew how to shop and she was thrifty about it. She could buy three articles of clothing and manage to get five outfits out of it.

We took our purchases and sat down at an outdoor café for some supper. By the time the sun had set, we arrived back at our apartment and that was when the trouble started.

"What the…" began Jackie as we walked through the door.

The place looked like it had been ransacked. The couch pillows had been thrown across the room. Our things were spread everywhere. In the kitchen, the cabinet doors hung open, which was odd since they had magnetic locks.

"What happened?" I breathed.

"Maybe the ghost did it," joked Jackie.

"Don't even," I scolded her. "I'm calling the cops."

The police arrived within thirty minutes. They took pictures, asked us if anything was stolen, and then left.

"Is that it?" I asked the uniformed officer as he walked out the door.

"There isn't much we can do, ma'am," he replied. "There have been a few burglaries in the area, but we haven't been able to catch the guys. I'm sure it won't happen again. Just keep the door locked."

Thanks for the advice, I thought as I closed the door behind him. "I can't believe he called me ma'am."

"I know," snickered Jackie. "You're an old mammy ma'am."

I smacked her with a pillow. "Help me clean this place up."

We spent the next several hours picking everything up and putting it back. Afterward, we both crashed on the couch and fell fast asleep.

Chapter 2

The next morning I woke with a start. Eight AM and I had an eight thirty class to get to. I jumped off the couch, knocking Jackie over.

"Hey," she whined.

I ignored her and quickly changed into some clean clothes, grabbed my keys, and ran out the door.

Luckily, the college wasn't far away and I was there in 15 minutes. I managed to squeak into the class just as the professor started speaking.

"Cutting it close," said the guy next to me as I slipped into a seat.

I just smiled in response and pulled out a notebook and pen. "Yeah, well, my alarm never went off."

"That's the problem with alarm clocks. My name is Greg Dotherson."

"Mellow Summers."

"Mellow."

"Most people call me Mel," I said. I couldn't stop staring at the man. He was beyond good looking and had perfect teeth.

"Well, Mel, nice to meet you."

"When you two are finished with your conversation, we'd like to continue." The professor's voice echoed through the room, effectively shutting us up. Apparently, we had interrupted his welcome to the class speech. Greg and I both turned toward the front, trying not to giggle. It was like being in high school all over again, including the stares.

The professor went on with his speech. His name was Professor Vincent. I just called him Vincent for short. For a guy in his forties, he was rather handsome as well. Hell, all these hot guys and I looked like I just crawled out of a garbage can. My self-consciousness made me miss most of Vincent's speech.

"Hey, it's time to go," said Greg, nudging my shoulder. "You look like you were a million miles away."

I gathered my stuff and left with Greg.

"You from around here?" asked Greg.

"No, I moved here to go to school," I replied. "I worked at a diner after high school graduation to save some money for college. And now, here I am."

"You live on campus?"

"No."

"I'm not trying to pry."

"With all these questions," I said.

"Okay. Maybe I was prying a little."

"I live in the Alamont Apartments with my friend Jackie."

"Really? That's where I live."

"Now you're pulling my leg," I said.

"No, I'm not. I swear," Greg said. "I'm thirty and I finally got around to getting my college degree. I don't care for the rowdiness of the dorms so I got an apartment at the Alamont. Second floor, number 215."

I couldn't believe it. He lived in number 215 right across the hall from me. What are the chances? "My apartment is 214."

"The dead girl's place?"

"You're not going to tell me it's haunted too are you?"

"No, it's just that place has sat empty more often than it's been occupied," said Greg. "The landlord has had some difficulty renting it. Not everyone wants an apartment that was formerly occupied by someone who was murdered. And tenants in there never stay very long."

"She wasn't killed inside it!"

"No, no. Her body was found on campus. But people get superstitious."

"Tell me about the girl," I asked, my curiosity getting the better of me.

"Her name was Rachel. Nice girl, but she could get a bit wild. Anyway, come October it will have been a year since her murder. The police never found out who did it and so no arrests were made. It's just become a cold case file.

"It's too bad, too, because she had a lot going for her. She was getting ready to graduate with her degree when it happened."

Suddenly, I felt sorry for this Rachel. And somewhat guilty for taking what had been her apartment. I checked my watch and realized I was late for my next class. What a great start I was off to this semester. "I need to run," I said, "but it was nice meeting you. Perhaps I'll see you around."

It was well past suppertime by the time I walked into the apartment. The smell of spaghetti and garlic bread greeted me. Jackie had dinner all prepared. I sat down at the table and reveled in the aroma of a good meal. "This is good," I said as I dug into the pasta.

"Guess what? I have a surprise." Jackie jumped up and down with excitement. Apparently, she had been waiting all day for me to get home. "I got a job!"

"So soon? How'd you do it?"

"Well, I walked into this shop, and this guy was making a fuss. Anyway, I told him to shut his mouth and be more polite. I was probably more forceful than necessary. Anyway, the manager saw the whole thing and hired me on the spot. I am now a sales clerk."

I just shook my head. Only Jackie could kick someone's butt and get a job out of the deal. "How much does it pay?"

"Ten bucks an hour and it's fulltime so I get benefits. Plus, the manager said that if I knew a friend who needed a job to bring them by. So you and me got jobs."

"What about my classes?" I asked.

"Taken care of," said Jackie as though I had asked a stupid question. "I told him that you were attending classes at the university. He said it was no problem. On the days you don't have school, you can work. Our pay will be enough to cover expenses."

I had to hand it to Jackie. We've only been here for two days and already she found us both jobs. But, she has always been good at getting what she wants. "Where are we working?"

"At the Candle Shoppe. We drove past it yesterday."

"You're a piece of work."

"So what did you do today?"

"Well, I met this guy."

"And you thought I'd been busy," said Jackie. "Is he cute? Did you ask him out?"

"One at a time." I held up my hand to stop her questioning. "Yes, he is very cute and he lives right across the hall from us, in apartment 215."

"No way," Jackie exclaimed.

"Way," I said. "He told me about the girl that used to live here."

"Oh, yeah?"

"Yeah, her name was Rachel and she went to the college here in town. She was killed last October. Her body was found on campus and the police never found out who murdered her."

"That's a bummer," said Jackie with her mouth full of garlic bread. "You sure you want to stay here?"

"I'm sure I'll be fine. Besides, it happened almost a year ago. What could possibly happen to me?"

"That is your first mistake. Never ask the 'what can go wrong' question. Anyway, I'm off to the shower. I have an early day tomorrow and so do you."

I continued eating my spaghetti after Jackie left. I heard the water turn on and figured she was right. I should think about going to bed. I cleaned up the dishes and put them in the sink. When I turned around, I nearly screamed. Standing before me was a woman of about my height, black skin and gorgeous black braids. She wore knee high boots, a knee length skirt, and a short sleeve, belted jacket.

"How did you get in here?" I demanded.

Instantly, the woman vanished. I couldn't believe my eyes. Had I just seen a ghost?

A knock sounded at the door. I jumped. Cautiously, I opened the door and there stood Greg, holding a platter with a cake on it. It was Devil's Food Cake, one of my favorites, and it had a rose decoration on it.

"I, uh, got in a baking mood and ended up baking a bunch of cakes. Since most people like chocolate, I thought maybe you might want one."

I took the cake, still speechless from my ghost encounter just a moment ago. "Thanks," I said.

"And I was wondering if you wanted to go out sometime."

Unfortunately, his question didn't register and I ended up closing the door in his face. I put the cake on the counter, still wondering what had just happened.

"Well that was wonderful," said a voice behind me.

Startled, I whirled around. The same woman had just reappeared. "Who are you?"

"Rachel. And this was my apartment," said the woman. "I can't believe you! A man brings you a cake with a rose and you slam the door in his face."

"What?"

"He was trying to ask you out, you dummy."

Suddenly, I remembered the cake and Greg asking me on a date. I ran to the door and flung it open. Of course, he wasn't there.

"Well, go knock on his door."

"You still here?" I said.

"I never left," said Rachel with her arms folded. "Go on. Apologize to him."

What if—," my words were cut off as Rachel shoved me toward Greg's door. I crashed into it with a loud bang. Suddenly, I had a headache. My knee throbbed as well.

The door opened and there stood Greg. God, he was gorgeous.

"Greg, I, umm, I'm sorry about earlier. Before you knocked on my door something had startled me and I guess I was still freaked when you asked me out. I'd love to go on a date with you, if you still want to."

"You like Mexican?" he said with a smile.

Hell, yes, I did. I'd like anything as long as he served it. "I love Mexican," I said, practically melting.

"Seven o'clock okay with you?"

"I'll be waiting."

"It's a date," said Greg. He closed the door and I went back to my apartment.

"Just throw yourself at him," said Rachel.

"What?" I just stood there looking like an idiot.

"By the way, you're welcome. And you might want to find a really nice outfit and wipe that stupid expression off your face." Rachel dissolved into thin air.

I couldn't believe it. Not only did I just speak with a ghost, but she helped me get a date, and then proceeded to offer me fashion advice. Could this day get any more interesting?

Chapter 3

"It is ten o'clock in the morning and is a bright sunny day. Be sure to wear a sweater when you go outside, for it is a bit chilly. Now, I believe it is time to... **get your lazy butt out of bed**!"

I groaned as I rolled over onto my side. I opened my eyes. Rachel stood over me. "Oh, no," I said, "it wasn't a dream?"

"Sorry, sweet cheeks," said Rachel, "but it all happened."

Ten o'clock, I thought. My class! I bolted out of bed and then realized that I had no classes today. I stood up and went to the bathroom. "I have to get to work and I don't need your assistance in the shower."

"I'm not into that kinky stuff." Rachel glanced down at my bare legs. "However, you might want to shave those hairy things before your date tonight."

I slapped my forehead. That's right! I had a date and, no, I hadn't shaved for several weeks. It was too much work and I preferred jeans anyway. I grabbed a towel and slammed the door in Rachel's face. "Good-bye," I said to her.

The Candle Shoppe was a nice little store. Despite its name, it had more than just candles. There were accessories, books, scent warmers, incense, and even handmade scarves. The soft lighting in the place provided a calm atmosphere for shopping. I loved it. It was much better than the harsh light of florescent bulbs. Candles littered the place with their flames. A great way to showcase the product.

The manager's name was Harvey Stilton. I just called him Mr. Stilton. He gave me a nametag, I filled out some paperwork, and he explained my duties. Jackie was already there helping customers. My job was managing the cash register, assisting customers, and restocking shelves.

My first day at work remained uneventful, for the most part. At least, it did, until Rachel showed up. I had an hour to go before my shift ended and she popped in.

"Hey," she said as she appeared next to me. Her voice startled me, causing me to send the tea lights in my hands flying across the store. I quickly retrieved them.

"What are you doing here?" I hissed at her.

"I just wanted to know how your first day at work is going," replied Rachel.

"I'm trying to work," I cut myself off as a couple people walked by. They looked at me strangely. My smile did little to assure them that I wasn't crazy. "You can't just show up when it pleases you. Now go away!"

"All right, fine," said Rachel. "I just thought you'd like to know that that guy over there is trying to make off with a bunch of merchandise." She disappeared.

I glanced over at the man she had pointed out. Sure enough, he stuffed his pockets with candles and incense. Figures. My first day and I get a shop lifter. I walked over to the man.

"Hey," I said. "You going to pay for that?"

He shoved me out of the way and bolted for the door. I tried going after him, but was too slow and ended up tripping over my own feet. Rachel appeared at the entrance and kicked him in the gut. The guy doubled over, allowing me to grab him.

"What's going on here?" demanded Mr. Stilton as he walked out of his office.

"Shoplifter," I said.

"Really?" Mr. Stilton emptied the man's pockets. "Go on get out of here," he said to the man. "If you ever come back here I'll call the cops."

The guy ran out the door. No doubt he was still wondering what hit him.

"You're welcome," said Rachel as she disappeared again. I was beginning to regret coming to Vermont.

Later that evening, I prepared for my date. Greg picked me up. I borrowed Jackie's floral, knee-length skirt and paired it with my new blouse and jacket she had bought me. I must admit, it looked good. The Mexican place was an outdoor restaurant. Despite the chill, we managed to stay fairly warm, thanks to the heating lamps they had.

"So," said Greg, "back story."

"You go first," I said.

"As I've said, I'm thirty and decided to finally go to college. I moved here a year ago and am studying criminology."

"Which explains why you are taking a video editing class."

"That is an elective I chose to take to fill some credits. And it's an easy A."

"Ah," I said. "I am hoping to be an independent filmmaker. Hence, why I am in Mr. Vincent's video editing class."

"So, the great Mellow Summers wishes to be an Oscar nominee."

"I was thinking more of an Oscar winner," I said.

The waiter brought our food. I dug into mine immediately after realizing how hungry I really was.

"I like a girl with a healthy appetite," said Greg. He watched me stuff a burrito in my mouth. Suddenly, I blushed. So much for first impressions.

"Can you tell me anymore about this Rachel?" I asked.

"Why do you want to know? You aren't saying your place is haunted are you?"

"There's just been little things," I said, hoping to brush aside his comments. Now that Rachel seemed to be making a habit of showing up wherever I was, I wanted to know more about her.

"There isn't much to tell," said Greg. "She kept to herself, mostly. However, she did like to frequent the bars. Especially this one place on the corner of Rhinestone and Main. It's called Zappy's."

"Zappy's?"

"Yeah. Strange name I know, but very popular among

the college crowd. There were many times she came home drunk and I'd have to help her unlock her door. But all that started to change when she met Tom. She stopped going to parties and stayed with him all the time.

"Her death really is a mystery. No one knows who would want to kill her. The cops focused on Tom at first, but with a lack of evidence, they had to let him go."

"Do you think he did it?" I asked.

"No," replied Greg. "He was a nice guy. Full ride scholarship and he worked at the local coffee shop. When he received the news of Rachel's death, it devastated him. When everything quieted down, he left. Too many people thought he did it and the damage had been done. Once labeled a suspect, it stays with you."

"I suppose it does. So, you never knew Rachel?"

"Not really well. Like I said, I saw her a few times and helped her into her apartment when she came home wasted, but we were more acquaintances. She seemed like a really nice girl, and, like I said, she did stop her drunken homecomings after meeting Tom. After that they were inseparable.

"For the most part Rachel kept to herself. Though there was this one night she came home in a panic."

"Panic?" I hoped the intrigue in my voice went unnoticed.

"It seemed that way. I remember her running to her apartment door. Her hair was frazzled and her clothes were disheveled. Her hands shook, too. I remember that because she had difficulty getting the key into the lock. I helped her open her door and asked if there was anything I could do. She said 'no' and so I left her alone."

"What happened after that?"

"Before I closed the door to my apartment, I over-heard her try to call Tom. Apparently, she had gotten his voicemail because she left a hurried message. Then she ran out of her apartment, got in her car, and left."

"What was the message?"

"The bit I heard was something about her catching something on camera. Something horrible, and she needed Tom's help. She did mention that she was head-ed to the computer lab on campus. That was the last time I saw her. The next morning, I learned that she had been killed."

"Her camera?"

"Yeah," said Greg. "She was taking the video ed-iting class as an elective as well. Apparently, making short movies was a hobby of hers. Anyway, her camera was never found and there was no evidence to indicate who killed her. Of course, the cops were so focused on Tom, that I don't think they even looked at anybody else. Though there was a Detective Shorts—"

"Shorts?" I didn't mean to interrupt, but the name sound-ed funny.

"Yeah, it is a funny name, but don't tell him that. You don't want to be on his bad side. He didn't think Tom did it. In fact, he seemed to think that someone who worked at the college did, but again, there was no proof."

"Too bad."

"Why all the questions? Here we are on a date and all I've done is talk about a dead girl."

I squirmed uneasily in my chair. Should I tell him

that I spoke with Rachel's spirit? It sounded so crazy that even I wasn't sure I believed it. "Just a few strange things have happened in my apartment that's all."

Greg laughed. "You're not going to tell me that you think your place is haunted!"

"I don't know." I wanted to end the conversation. This was only a first date and to tell Greg I was seeing a ghost wasn't in the plan. "It's getting late," I said.

Greg agreed and asked for the check, which he paid. That impressed me. Afterward, he walked me home and dropped me off at my apartment. We didn't kiss or anything. In fact, we just said good-bye.

After I let myself in, I slumped down on the couch. I had a real mystery on my hands. You know, that thing you mostly read about in novels, or watch on TV. I felt like Jessica Fletcher from *Murder She Wrote*. I just couldn't stop thinking about it. Why was Rachel afraid? What was she running from? And who killed her? Then it occurred to me that I had all the answers at my fingertips.

"Rachel," I whispered.

"How was the date?" She appeared on the couch beside me.

"It was great," I replied.

"Did you kiss?"

"Uh, no."

She let out an exasperated sigh. "Going to play hard to get. I don't get you."

I shook my head. The conversation was not going where I wanted it to. "Rachel," I said, "who killed you? I mean, what happened that night you died?"

I thought she might be upset at my abruptness, but instead she seemed pleased that someone asked. "I don't know," she said.

"You don't know?"

"I can't remember. People think that when you die you suddenly know everything. But that didn't happen to me. I remember bits and pieces, but nothing substantial. Mostly, I remember being scared and running for my life and then I ended up here. People went right past me. They couldn't see me, or hear me."

"Why is it I can see you?" I really wanted to know why I suddenly became Jessica Love-Hewitt from *Ghost Whisperer.*

"I learned much later that I can decide who sees me and who doesn't. But I also learned that most people pretend not to see ghosts. Either that, or they are so wrapped up in their own life, that they ignore everything that doesn't immediately affect them.

"Some of the people who lived here before you saw me, but they either passed it off as being crazy, or they just ran away scared. I wasn't trying to scare anyone. I just wanted to be heard. I also want to know what happened to me. But I need someone living to help."

"But you can go anywhere you want and spy on people," I said.

"But I can't talk to them. I'm not sure why I'm able to talk to you. It could be because you haven't run off scared yet. Will you help me?"

I sighed. I wanted to. And I was curious. The fact that her murder has remained unsolved meant that that the real killer was still at large. I shuddered at the thought. "I don't know."

"Please," she begged. "I need to know what happened."

I sat silent for a while. I did want to know what happened to her, but I also didn't want to do anything to ruin my new start in life. In the end, I relented. "Yes, I'll help. But you have to promise to quit showing up unannounced."

"Yay!" squealed Rachel, jumping up and down.

A part of me felt that I would regret this.

Chapter 4

Three weeks passed, and before I knew it, I had buried myself under a mountain of homework. Who knew that college could be this difficult? I had spent each day since my date with Greg scurrying around on campus between classes, darting back and forth from work, and getting home late with just enough time to sleep.

Greg and I continued seeing each other. When not in class, we met for coffee or lunch. I only saw Jackie a few times, mostly when at work. Unfortunately, I hadn't had time to really investigate Rachel's death. Rachel's insistence at showing up whenever she liked didn't help. I had a feeling this was going to be a common occurrence with her.

The weather had turned a bit colder as we moved into

October. I was glad that Jackie had bought me that jacket. It was quite warm.

I jogged across campus with my arms full of books. One more class to go today and I could go home. The late afternoon sun felt nice, but I hadn't time to enjoy it.

"Mel!" Once again Rachel appeared from nowhere.

Her sudden appearance caused me to drop my books. They scattered everywhere. "Rachel, not now," I said. I knelt down to gather my stuff.

"Have you found any leads?"

"I'm sorry, no. I've been busy."

"But you said you would help me," whined Rachel.

"Rachel, I will help, but you need to give me something to go on. Right now, I'm about as far as the cops got. Now, please, go away. I have a class to get to. We can talk later when I get home."

A couple of people walked by. I continued picking up my books and tried to ignore them. "Please, Rachel," I whispered. "If I stand here talking to you, people will think I'm crazy."

"Oh, please," replied Rachel, "you're way past that. You agreed to help a ghost find her murderer."

"Rachel, you can't keep popping in when you please. You may be dead, but I have responsibilities. Now go back to the apartment and I'll meet you there."

More people walked by. They stared at me with a questioning look.

"Practicing for a play," I said with a smile. Their glances told me that they didn't buy it.

"Fine. If I go back, do you promise to spend the night with me, helping me figure out who killed me?"

"Yes."

With that, Rachel left. I grabbed the rest of my things and hurried off to the other end of campus for my math class.

I arrived home to find Rachel waiting for me. She sat on the couch, watching television. She snapped her fingers and the TV turned off. Luckily, Jackie had to work, so I didn't need to worry about her walking in while I talked with a ghost.

"So, how was school?" asked Rachel.

I dropped my books and slumped in a chair, exhausted. I had a mountain of homework, but it would have to wait. Right now, it was time for Rachel and I to talk. I had promised her and guessed I ought to quit putting it off.

"The usual," I responded to her question.

"Well," Rachel jumped to her knees on the couch, "It's time to put all that aside and concentrate on catching my murderer."

I thought about her statement a moment. A part of me thought that it sounded selfish. I pushed it aside. I did promise to help her, and right now it was all about her.

"What do you remember about the night you died?" I asked.

Rachel rubbed her chin, concentrating. "Most of it is a blur. I remember I had a night class that night. It was the usual three hours of boredom, but I got through it. Afterward, I went to Zappy's to meet with some friends."

"Greg said you came home late in a panic. That you rummaged in your apartment for something, called Tom, and left," I said.

"That's right, I did! But I don't remember what had frightened me," said Rachel.

"What class was it?"

"Huh?"

"You're night class. What was it?"

"It was that video editing class with Professor Vincent," replied Rachel.

I massaged my temples. This was going nowhere. I had a ghost that only I could speak to who wanted help finding her murderer. The only problem was she couldn't remember the night she died.

"Are any of your friends still at the college?" I asked.

"Most of them graduated last May," replied Rachel. Suddenly, she jumped up in excitement. "Sara! Sara is still there. She failed a couple of her classes and was forced to stay an extra semester. She and I were pretty close—like sisters!"

"It's a start."

"We should go see her right now."

I stared at Rachel. "Now? It's nine o'clock at night. I'm tired and want some sleep."

"Which is why this is the perfect time to go. She'd be at Zappy's. It's a great place to hang out, for college kids."

"But it's in the middle of the week," I protested. I had no desire to go anywhere. I just wanted to go to bed.

"Like that's ever stopped any one from going to the bar. Come on, party pooper." Rachel hauled me out of my comfortable chair. Before I knew it my purse and keys were shoved into my hands and I was out the door.

I drove across town, following Rachel's directions to Zappy's. I cranked my radio up so no one would wonder why I seemed to be talking to myself. When I pulled into Zappy's parking lot, I had to drive around to find a parking space. The crowd was unbelievable! Ten minutes later, I finally found a space to park the car. The music pounded against the windows.

"Let's find her quick," I told Rachel.

Secretly, I hoped that she wouldn't be there. I had no idea what I would say without coming across as an amateur sleuth; or just plain nosy. I chuckled inside. That's exactly what I was.

A wave of tobacco smoke, booze, and pounding music wafted over me. I detested these places. Yet, I had to be here to help Rachel get her memory back.

"I.D.?"

I stared at the guy behind the counter for a moment until I realized that he was talking to me. I quickly handed him my driver's license. He looked it over, frowned, and handed it back. Apparently, he was hoping to bust some high school student trying to sneak in.

"Five bucks," said the guy.

"What?"

"Five dollar cover charge," he repeated.

Luckily, I had some cash with me. I forked over a five and went in. Instantly, I understood why this was a college hangout. The loud music and alcohol was an open invitation for it; but the place had a private section for those who wanted to be alone, a dance floor, and a bar with stools. I picked a menu off of a table and glanced at it in the multicolored lighting. They served food as well.

"Wheee!" shouted Rachel next to me. "This is fun isn't it?"

"Hey," I shouted at her, "we're here to work. Remember?"

"Sorry," said Rachel, "it's been awhile since I felt alive—so to speak."

"Do you see her?" I glanced around at the crowd. The place was packed. No way were we going to find Sara in here.

"No," said Rachel. "Stay here while I look around." She left me alone. I glanced around me. Without any ideas on what to do, I meandered to the bar.

"What'll it be?" asked the bartender.

I racked my brain trying to remember the list of drinks. "Southern Tropics." Instantly, my drink appeared and I had to hand over some money. I raised my drink to my lips.

"Hey!"

Rachel popped out of nowhere and grabbed my shoulder. I dropped my drink. Great. Instead of drinking my beverage, I was wearing it. I snatched some paper napkins and attempted, in vain, to wipe the mess off my jacket.

"I found her," said Rachel.

"Where is she?"

"Up there on the second floor," replied Rachel.

"Hey, baby."

I turned around and found a man ogling me. The man's breath stank of too much liquor. I ignored him.

"Hey," he persisted, "I said 'hi'!"

"Kick him in the nuts," said Rachel.

I shook my head. I didn't want trouble and having two people talk to me at the same time was very confusing. "Go away, please," I said to the guy next to me.

He grabbed my shoulder and whirled me around to face him. "I don't like being ignored," he spat.

I struggled to break free, but his grasp was too strong. Before I knew it, Rachel had appeared by his side. She yanked his stool out from under him, causing the man to bang his head on the counter.

"Hey, bitch," said the man as he stood up.

Rachel snatched a beer bottle off the counter. The man stared in horror as it floated towards him, clonking him on his skull. He ran off, knocking tables and chairs over. I stared aghast at what just happened. A few people eyed me peculiarly. I waved at them. Instantly, Rachel grabbed my arm, pulling me from the bar.

"You need to be more forceful," she scolded me.

"Look what you did," I said in shock.

"Oh, he'll be alright," she said passing off my concerns as little importance. "When a guy won't leave you alone, you don't politely ask them to leave. You force them to go away."

"My mother always said that girls should be sugar and spice and everything nice. You know, like that poem."

Rachel looked at me as though I had just told her I had seen Bigfoot. "You're kidding, right?" she said. "In this place, sometimes you have to be sugar and spice and not so nice. Come on."

We reached the top of the steps. The music wasn't quite so loud up here. I glanced around at all the people in the booths. Some were couples, but most were groups of friends out for a good time.

"There she is," Rachel said, pointing to a girl in her early twenties. She had shoulder length, blonde hair with red highlights. Thankfully, she seemed to be alone. I weaved my way through the tables and booths towards Sara.

"Hi," I greeted her. "My name's Mel."

She put her drink down. "Sara," she said, "Nice to meet you. First time here?"

"Yeah." I helped myself to a seat. "I just moved here for school."

"Welcome to Vermont," Sara said. "You'll be coming here often, I'm sure. Everyone does."

"You here alone?" I asked.

"Am now. I came with some people but they wanted to go to an after party. I figured I'd finish my drink and go home. You live on campus?"

I couldn't believe my luck. Sara had just given me the perfect opening. "I moved into the Alamont Apartments, not far from campus. Apartment 214."

"Rachel's place," said Sara. She set her drink on the table. "Why'd you move there?"

"I'm sorry," I said, "Cheap rent and furnished. I didn't know about Rachel until after I signed the lease."

"Don't worry about it," apologized Sara, "Of course, you didn't know. It was a place to rent. And who wouldn't at the price they were offering?"

"Did you know Rachel well?"

"We were good friends," said Sara. "Rachel was always fun to be around. This was our favorite place to hang out."

I tried to think of a way to ease into questioning about the night Rachel died. I couldn't, so I just jumped into it. "I hear the cops never found who killed her."

"No. Those bastards. They didn't even try."

Clearly, Sara thought that the entire case had been mishandled. That boded well for me.

"They focused on Tom, but that guy couldn't hurt a fly. He was one of those rare ones that is a genuine gentleman, and isn't gay."

I nodded my head in understanding at that last statement.

"Tom loved Rachel. And she loved him. I mean, they were truly in love. They had just gotten engaged two days before. No one knew, but me. No, Tom wasn't the type. Naturally, there was no evidence for a conviction and the cops let the case drop because they were too lazy to reconsider their list of suspects, or suspect.

"Poor Tom," Sara continued, "He was devastated by Rachel's death. The constant bombardment by the cops ruined his life here. Afterward, everyone thought he had done it. He packed up and left when the investigation ended. Didn't even wait for the semester to end."

"And no one's heard from him since?" I asked.

"Nope. He left no forwarding address. Said he didn't want anything to do with this place. Can't blame him. His life here ended when Rachel died."

"Poor guy," I said. "But who would have killed her?"

"Don't know. Rachel was with me, here, that night. We had a night class together and usually came here for a little bit afterwards. I remember her leaving at around midnight. She went to her car and that was the last I saw her. An hour later, I got a call from Tom. He said she had left him a cryptic voice message. Something about witnessing a terrible act and needing his help to email a video. She wasn't the most technologically advanced person. Anyway, he said she wanted to meet him in the computer lab at the college. He got the message late, and when he arrived, she wasn't there."

"Why wouldn't she be there?"

"You know, you're asking a lot of questions. You aren't one of those crime junkies that get their kicks prying into unsolved murders, are you?"

"No, I just have a natural curiosity."

"Yeah, sure you do." Sara stood up. "Look, I don't know you and I don't feel right talking about Rachel's death to a stranger. Leave me alone."

"You can't let her leave," said Rachel. "Call her a 'fat chick'. Quick!"

"Fat Chick!" I yelled it out loud and everyone turned in my direction.

Sara paused, glaring at me questioningly. Then, she went down the stairs and my chance of getting more information was over.

I rested my face in my hands in exasperation. "That went well," I said. "You want to tell me why I just called a complete stranger a 'fat chick'?"

Rachel sat across from me with a disappointed look

on her face. "That was a saying between the two of us. It was something only she and I used. She had to know it came from me. But she's right. We did come here that night. We were celebrating my recent engagement. I can't believe that I'd forgotten that. Poor Tom! The police thought it was him?"

"So he didn't kill you?" I asked.

"Tom? No!" Rachel stared at me as though I had just eaten a rock off the ground. "Tom was the first man to treat me like a lady. He never raised his voice at me, or threaten me. Even when I lost my temper at him, he would just calmly reassure me that everything would be alright. He always did little things for me. You know, the chores that no one wants to do. He did them so that I wouldn't have to get my hands dirty. No, Mel, Tom didn't kill me. Of that I'm certain. I miss him."

Rachel started to cry. I felt sorry for her. She had died soon after getting engaged to a great guy. On top of that, the cops failed to find her killer and almost ruined her fiancé's life. My heart ached for her sadness. Is this what it was like to die? To linger on, alone, while those you loved carried on with their lives?

"Rachel," I soothed, "I'm sorry. We'll find the truth. We will."

Someone cleared their throat next to me. The waitress had walked up and I never noticed. I looked at her sheepishly, wondering how long she had been there listening to me basically talk to myself. "A beer please," I said.

The waitress eyed the empty glasses that littered the table. Naturally, she thought that they were all mine.

"You don't think I drank all of these," I blurted out, "These aren't mine!"

"Uh-huh," said the waitress with her hands on her hips. "Honey, anyone who talks to themselves is either drunk, or crazy. Considering there are all these empty glasses, I figure it's the former. I think it's time you went home."

I scowled at Rachel. She laughed out loud, but, unsurprisingly, only I heard her. I stood up and sauntered toward the stairs.

"Make sure someone drives you home," said the waitress after me.

I made it to the main floor without too much incident. Once again, I weaved my way through throngs of people who busied themselves with having a good time. I had almost made it to the exit when a big, burly man stood in my way. Leather and tattoos covered his dark skin. I tried to go around him. It was no use. He kept blocking me.

"Excuse me," I said.

"You one fine honey," growled the man.

Oh no, I thought. Here we go again.

"How about you and me leaving this place?"

"Some other time," I said. I didn't like what he had in mind.

The man inched closer. I held my breath to keep from passing out from his stench. I backed away, but a table blocked my progress.

"Knee him in the stomach and bash his face in," instructed Rachel.

"What?" I replied.

The man bent down to kiss me. This time, I did as Rachel suggested. I rammed my knee hard into the man's soft middle. Then, I broke his nose with the heel of my hand. Afterward, I managed to wrench his arm behind his back and bashed his face into the table. The man fell to the floor in agony.

His friends stared at me in shock. I glanced around at all of them not believing what I had just done.

"Anyone else want some?" I said, sounding braver than I felt.

No one moved.

"Time to leave," said Rachel.

Quickly, I dashed out the exit into the chilly night air. I inhaled deeply to clear out my lungs before I got in my car and drove home.

"I didn't know you had that in you," squealed Rachel with laughter. "Dang, girl, you broke his nose on top of that! You are a tough cookie."

The adrenaline of knocking that guy down eventually wore off. I laughed with Rachel. Even I had difficulty believing that I had done that.

"That is what I'm talking about," Rachel continued. "Sometimes you have to show a guy that no means no. And if that means dealing out a few bruises, then so be it. You may learn a thing or two from me yet."

We laughed and giggled the rest of the way home. I finally walked through the door to the apartment at around two in the morning. My eyes barely stayed open long enough for me to make it to my room and crawl into bed.

Chapter 5

It seemed as though I had just fallen asleep when I woke up. Daylight peeked through the curtains in my room. Seven in the morning. I rolled over and tried to go back to sleep. Sleep was to be denied to me though.

Jackie burst through the door to my room. "Where were you?" she demanded. "You weren't here when I got home. And then you didn't come crawling in until two in the morning!"

I just glowered at her. "What are you, my mother?"

"I was worried about you. It's not like you to go off like that."

"I just needed to go out for a bit," I said. My explanation did little to assuage Jackie. I didn't know my going to the bar with Rachel would alarm her.

"Right," said Jackie, "Well, get up. I'll make breakfast. We can go to work together."

I crawled out of bed, wishing I could go back to sleep. Drowsily, I went to the bathroom.

"Hey!" Once again Rachel popped in expecting me to drop everything as though I had nothing better to do.

"Rachel," I yawned, "if you don't mind, I'd like to shower in peace."

"I realize that," said Rachel, "but I might have remembered something."

I ran my fingers through my hair, not paying any attention to what she said. "That's great."

I stifled another yawn. I glanced toward the end of the hallway. Jackie stood there gaping at me.

"Are you okay?" she asked.

Instead of answering, I slammed the door to the bathroom.

"We'll talk later," Rachel shouted through the door.

Work was unusually busy when Jackie and I arrived. I went to the cashier station and placed my stuff behind the counter. The line of people making purchases slowly grew smaller. I glanced around as I rung up people's things. Jackie was involved with a difficult lady who insisted that the sage incense did not smell like sage.

Only one other person wandered the floor. Charlie. The man was useless. He loved the paycheck, but did everything he could to keep from working. True to his past, Charlie disappeared as more people walked through the door.

I don't know why Mr. Stilton hired him. Maybe it

was because the two were a lot alike. Mr. Stilton spent most of his time in his office with the door closed. I sighed. It looked like Jackie and I would be running the place again.

"Thirteen, sixty-five," I said to the man in front of me. He paid his bill quickly and walked out the door without so much as a smile. People are so rude sometimes. "Next," I called.

Before I could even greet the elderly lady in front of me, Jackie grabbed my arm and pulled me to the floor behind the counter. "Jackie…" I began.

She shushed me. "Don't move," she whispered. "There's this guy that keeps coming in here asking for you. I think he might be a stalker. Look."

She pointed the man out to whom she referred. I peeked around the corner of the counter. I'm sure that the people waiting to pay for their stuff thought we were nuts. I clapped my hand over my mouth, stifling a laugh when I noticed who it was.

"That's Greg," I told Jackie. "The guy I have been dating."

"That's him?" She peered at him, taking in all of his features. "He's cute. I approve." Jackie jumped to her feet, "Greg," she yelled across the store, "your girl-friend's over here."

Humiliated, I gradually rose to my feet. "Greg," I said, trying to sound like everything was normal. I didn't want to know what he was thinking.

"You always hide behind the counter?" he asked.

"Hide?" I stammered. "I wasn't hiding, I was… uh… looking for something."

Greg gave me one of those "I don't believe you" looks. He must think I'm crazy. "There is a performance at the theater tonight. I have tickets and wanted to know if you were up for it."

"Oh? What's playing?"

"Hamlet."

I almost dropped my jaw. A guy who was into Shakespeare? I couldn't believe it. Either that, or he somehow found out that I loved Shakespeare. "I'd love to go."

"Perfect," said Greg. "I'll pick you up when you get off work."

Jackie and I watched him leave. She smiled broadly, shaking my shoulder in excitement that I finally got a boyfriend. Then, I remembered the giant line of people at the counter staring at me. My face flushed red from embarrassment. Great, now the world knows about my love life.

"He's hot."

I turned toward the voice. It belonged to the old lady that was next in line.

"If I were you," she began, "I would hold onto him tightly. In fact, if I were sixty years younger I'd squeeze his butt cheeks tight."

I gawked at her in disbelief. Jackie stood next to me, trying not to burst out laughing. So was everyone else in line. I could just imagine what my face looked like. I rung up her items quickly. "Fourteen dollars even."

She handed me exact change and left. At the door, the woman turned and waved at me with a huge grin, and left.

"So are you going to squeeze his butt cheeks?" asked Rachel, standing by the shelves behind me.

Without thinking, I grabbed a small candle and chucked it at her. Of course, it did no good. It passed right through her, and to everyone else, it looked as though I had thrown it at thin air.

I smiled sheepishly at those watching me. "Uh, I saw a bug," I said in an effort to explain my actions.

They just grinned in that way people do when they think you're off your rocker, but they don't want to say anything.

Someone placed more things on the counter. They landed with a soft thump. Automatically, I typed in their prices. Black votive candles, incense, and aromatherapy oils. "$25.69," I said.

That's when I saw who it was that was in front of me: Professor Vincent. Though he wasn't the first guy to buy things like this, I thought it odd that he would.

"Mellow, right?" he said.

"It's Mel," I replied.

The man handed me thirty dollars and I gave him his change.

"I would never peg you as someone who was into all this aromatherapy stuff," I said. I don't know why I did. I guess my natural curiosity took over.

"I suffer from migraines," he said, "and this stuff seems to help."

I gave him my clerk smile in response. In the back of my mind, his explanation sounded like a lie. But, why would he lie? Even if he was, what business was it of mine anyway?

"You're in my video editing class," said Professor Vincent.

I thought it odd that he'd ask such a question. He knew I was in his class. I sat right in front of him. "Yes," I replied.

"I thought so," he said, "I liked that last assignment you handed in. You have an artistic eye for things. I think you ought to consider signing up for my advanced film-making class next semester."

His statement sounded reasonable, but I started to feel uncomfortable around him. Especially since his eyes darted down my blouse.

"I'll think about it," I replied.

"Do that." Professor Vincent left. He gave me a lustful look, but did a good job at concealing it.

"Creepy bastard," said Jackie. She had observed the entire proceeding. "I'd drop his class."

"Except, I need the credits," I said.

"I guess the world is full of creeps like him," she said.

"I'll make certain to sit in the back of the class from now on," I told her.

"Do that."

Luckily, the rest of the day at work passed without incident. Things had quieted down considerably. Seven pm rolled around and Jackie and I had the honor of locking up. One of the things I liked about the Candle Shoppe was that is closed early.

Greg arrived right on time with flowers. Jackie beamed and nudged me when she saw him. "Flowers! How nice," she said. "Have fun." She greeted Greg and ran off.

Greg handed me the flowers and I accepted them graciously. He took me to an Italian restaurant for dinner. As I ate the delicious food, I knew it headed straight to my thighs. All that creamy, buttery pasta was too good to resist. We chit chatted at dinner, but I was so hungry, that I stuffed my face more than talk. Greg chuckled. At least my tendency to eat didn't scare him away.

The play started at nine and we had seats in the front. It gave us a perfect view of the stage. The moment the curtain went up, the actors and story enthralled me. Like I said, I love Shakespeare. Hamlet had always been one of my favorites. I don't know why. But who wouldn't like a story about a guy who seeks revenge for his father's death, and pretends to go crazy while he's at it? Though you could argue that Hamlet really was nuts. I understood how he felt. Ever since I met Rachel, I felt a little nutty myself. Hopefully, no one tried to put me in a padded cell.

The play ended at midnight and a giant yawn gave away my tiredness. It had been a long day and I looked forward to actually getting a good night's sleep. "Thanks for a wonderful night," I said to Greg.

He opened the door to his car for me. What a gentleman. I'll admit, that meant bonus points in my book. He drove me home. We didn't say much during the car ride. My eyelids kept drooping and he must have noticed. Afterward, he walked around the car to open my door for me. More bonus points. Some girls didn't like it when guys opened doors for them, but I didn't mind it once in a while.

"You make sure to go to bed," he said, dropping me off at my door.

"Don't worry," I said.

Then, he did it. Kissed me goodnight. It was one of those foot popping kisses that gave me butterflies. The kiss ended too quickly for me. I had to hide my girlish giggles as butterflies swirled in my stomach.

"Night," I said as I closed the door.

I dumped my things on a nearby chair.

"How was your date?" asked Jackie. She sat cross legged on the couch with a book in her hands. The eagerness in her voice tipped me off that she had been spying. That, and the fact that the book in her hands was upside down.

"You were watching through the peephole, weren't you?" I said.

"No... Me?" I didn't buy the forced innocence of her voice.

"I've never known anyone who could read upside down," I said.

Jackie slammed the book shut and hopped off the couch. "OK, so maybe I was being a little nosy."

"You're worse than my mother."

"Am not. So you kissed. Good news. You like him?"

"Of course I like him," I said. "He's a bit of a gentle-man. He doesn't like to party, or smoke. And that cake he gave us was delicious."

"So he can cook. If he does his own laundry, and starches his clothes, I'd say he's a keeper."

"I'm sure he's house trained," I said. "Now, I have an early class tomorrow, so if you don't mind, I'm going to bed."

Chapter 6

I strolled toward the building where my first class of the day was. October hit and with it came chilly weather. I knew I'd have to start searching for my winter coat soon, but kept putting it off. Despite being a warm weather type of gal, I relished in the cold breeze. Somehow, it made you feel alive.

I pulled the heavy door to the building open and enjoyed the warm air that engulfed me. For once, I felt good about going to class. No Rachel today, and I actually got some sleep.

I started to walk through the doorway to my video editing class when a hand seized my arm and yanked me away. I found myself being shoved and pushed down the hall toward the water fountains. It was Sara. She shoved me against the wall and motioned for me to be quiet.

"What the—"

"SHH!" Sara looked around making certain no one was watching. She relaxed and let me go. "I'm sorry," she said. "It's just I don't want anyone to know that I talked to you."

"I don't understand," I said. I really didn't want to be late for my class.

"When you asked me about Rachel the other night, I was afraid that I was being set up."

"Set up?"

"Look, when the cops focused on Tom as Rachel's killer, I knew they were going in the wrong direction," said Sara. "Tom wasn't the type. There was this one cop who was intent on nailing him. He didn't want to hear about anything else. His name was Detective Reiss. The thing is, the guy made me nervous. There was just something about him. You know how it is when you get a bad vibe about someone? That's what I got from that Reiss character."

"Why are you telling me this now?" I asked.

"I thought maybe you were sent by Reiss to spy on me. He did that for a while after the investigation closed. I freaked. But when you called me a 'fat chick', I knew you couldn't be from him. Where did you hear that term?"

"You wouldn't believe me if I told you," I said.

"Try me," Sara pushed.

I exhaled deeply. "Do you believe in ghosts?"

"Ghosts?"

"I told you, you wouldn't believe me," I said.

"You see ghosts?"

"Only one," I said. I knew she'd think I was definitely crazy for telling her this, but she asked. She made it evident that she wasn't going to let it go. "I've seen Rachel."

Sara's lips pursed. "I don't know if you're crazy, or lying, but I do know that there isn't any way you could have known that phrase."

"Rachel told it to me," I said.

"Fat chick. We used to say that to each other when we went out. It was our code for drop dead gorgeous. Seems stupid I know."

"Not at all," I said. "Sara, do you have any idea why Rachel was so scared that night? Or why she went to the computer lab so late?"

"I've no idea what could have scared her," replied Sara. "All I know is she called me saying something about taping something on her camera. Something horrible. She wouldn't give any details. She wanted me and Tom to meet her at the computer lab, which was open 24/7."

"She obviously needed a computer for something," I said more to myself than to Sara. "Why would she need a computer here on campus? Didn't she have her own?"

"Her computer was at a repair shop. It stopped working one day and she wasn't going to get it back for another week. Tom didn't own one and I didn't have internet at my place."

"But if she filmed some kind of crime, why wouldn't she go to the cops?"

"Maybe she felt she couldn't trust them. I know I didn't trust that Detective Reiss," said Sara. "Why do you want to know?"

"I made a promise to a friend," I said, "and I find it odd that it was closed so quickly and no one's given it much thought since. This happened on campus. That means the murderer could still be here." I immediately regretted saying that last bit. Sara's face filled with shock. She covered it up well.

"You're probably right," she said, "Listen, I came to the computer lab soon after getting her call. When I got here, it was empty, except for one person."

"Who?"

Sara glanced over and did a double take. Greg stood in the hallway watching us. "Him," she said, pointing to him. "Just find who did this. And be careful of Professor Vincent."

Sara left, leaving Greg and I alone in the empty hallway. "Greg," I said. He walked off. "Greg!" I yelled.

"What?" he said.

"You didn't tell me everything," I accused. "You told me that you last saw Rachel at her apartment, but the truth is you went to the computer lab. Why didn't you tell me?"

"What does it matter?"

"Why, Greg? If you can't be honest with me about that, how can I believe if anything you tell me is the truth?"

"Honesty," said Greg, "You want honesty? Why don't you tell me why you really want to know?"

"I don't like injustice," I said. It sounded stupid, even to my ears.

"There's more to it than that." Greg sauntered away.

"Why were you at the computer lab?" I demanded. "And why didn't you tell me?"

"I followed her, okay? Rachel was so frightened that night, that I was afraid for her. Afraid of what she might do. So I followed her. By the time I reached the computer lab, she had left. I noticed her leaving through the exit with someone, but before I could catch up with her, Sara arrived. When I did make it outside, she, and whoever she was with, had gone.

"I told the cops that. They just assumed the guy was Tom. Why do you keep pushing?"

"Because I've talked to Rachel. She asked my help in finding her killer and I agreed."

"Mel, just don't get involved. They didn't care then and they don't care now. You're just going to stir up a bunch of trouble and open old wounds."

"And maybe solve a murder while I'm at it." I left Greg standing there and went to my class. I knew I was late, but didn't care. I just walked in and took the closest available seat, ignoring the stares I got from those around me.

I barely paid attention in class. The teacher droned on and on about film technique and use of colors. My mind, however, lay elsewhere. All I thought about was what Sara told me, and later, Greg. I understood why he didn't tell me that last bit about following Rachel. It just hurt that he skewed the truth a bit. Didn't he trust me? Did I trust him?

The movement of people told me that class had ended. I grabbed my book bag and stood up to leave.

"Miss Summers," said Professor Vincent.

I approached the desk.

"I noticed you were late," he said, "I do not appreciate tardiness."

"Sorry, professor," I said, "It won't happen again."

"I'm sure it won't." Professor Vincent placed his smooth hand on my shoulder. I thought his eyes flickered toward my bosom. I suddenly felt very uncomfortable. "Be on time next time." His grin possessed a lustfulness.

"I have to go," I said and left.

The rest of my classes went quickly. I headed straight home. I didn't even remember the drive back to the apartment. I burst through the door actually hoping to see Rachel. She wasn't there.

"Rachel!" I yelled. "Rachel!"

"What," said Rachel from behind me.

"Can't you remember anything that happened to you that night? I feel like I'm going in circles."

"I'm sorry," said Rachel. "It's all fuzzy."

"Or, you don't want to remember." I regretted that statement the moment it exited my mouth.

"Don't want to? Do you think I like being here not knowing why or how I died?" Rachel glared at me. "Do you think this is fun for me?

"I was always told that when a person died they met God, or at least saw their loved ones again, but instead of any of that, I found myself back here. At first I didn't know I was dead, but I figured it out quickly when everyone I tried to talk to couldn't see, or hear, me. Those that did, ran away screaming.

"All I asked from you is a little help. And all you have done is complain."

"I am trying to help you, but everyone I talk to thinks I'm either crazy or nosy. And now my boyfriend has basically left me because I had to tell him why I am so interested in finding out what happened to you; and why I was upset that he didn't mention following you to the college."

"He what?" said Rachel.

"He followed you and saw you leaving with someone, but he doesn't know who. But it doesn't matter. He'll probably never speak to me again."

"Is that so?" Rachel vanished.

"Mel?" Jackie appeared in the doorway. She had a concerned look on her face. "What's going on?"

"Nothing," I said.

"Nothing?" Jackie's stance told me she didn't believe me. "Nothing. Ever since we moved here, you have acted strangely. Constantly late for things. Going out and staying out until all hours in the morning. Getting in a bar fight. And talking to yourself. Something is going on and I want to know what it is."

I stood awkwardly. I didn't want Jackie to think I had lost my mind, yet, I wanted her to know the truth. "You want the truth?"

"Mel, you can tell me anything."

"When we moved here, I met a ghost. But not any ghost. It's the spirit of the girl who lived here before us."

Jackie stared at me in disbelief. She didn't believe me. "A ghost. Mel, if you don't—"

A loud crash echoed across the hall. Jackie and I both ran to the hallway. More thumps and bangs sounded. We eyed each other, wondering what was happening. Greg's door opened. Out came Rachel, dragging Greg into our apartment. She stopped in our entrance. "Does this belong to you?"

I bursted out laughing. Jackie glanced from me to Rachel. Even Greg seemed uneasy. They saw Rachel too. Relief swept over me as now they had to believe me.

"I guess you were telling the truth about seeing a ghost," said Greg. Rachel dumped him on the floor.

"Rachel, why—"

"I can't have them putting you in a padded cell when I still need your help," Rachel said interrupting me.

"You mean," said Jackie, "that you weren't kidding?"

"No, she wasn't," said Rachel. "Now, I don't want to sit here answering questions. Mel agreed to help me find my murderer."

"I didn't… Rachel," said Greg.

"Relax," said Rachel. "I know it wasn't you."

"Do you know what could have been on that camera, or what you did with it?" I asked.

"No," said Rachel, exasperated.

"It's too bad we can't get a look at the police report," said Jackie.

Greg pulled out his cell phone. "I can help with that," he said. "I have a cousin who works at the local police department. He's a file clerk, but great at hacking." Greg dialed a number and put his phone on speaker.

"Hello," came a male voice on the line.

"Jack," said Greg, "I need a favor."

"No," said Jack. "No more favors. I can't. I could lose my job."

"Jack," Greg said, "you are indebted to me for life."

"Will you stop that?" The line went dead a moment. "Am I on speaker?"

"Yes," replied Greg, "and I still need that favor. Or do I need to tell your mother why you missed church last Sunday?"

"You wouldn't," came Jack's panicked voice.

"That favor?"

"Oh, all right," said Jack, "What do you need?"

"I need you to look up the file on that college girl who was murdered last year," said Greg.

A bunch of coughing filled the line. Jack must have choked when he heard Greg's request. "That case is closed."

"Jack, I have your mother on speed dial," threatened Greg.

"Okay. Okay. Give me a moment." A series of taps echoed through the line as Jack typed on the keyboard. "You realize I can get in a lot of trouble for this. Okay. Got it."

"What does it say? Is there an autopsy report?"

"She was found around dawn," said Jack. "She died from a blow to the head by a blunt object. The coroner figured it was made of wood because he pulled splinters from the wound. There were also signs of strangulation. DNA was pulled from under the fingernails, but was ruled inconclusive."

"Inconclusive?" I asked.

"Something about it being contaminated. The report is a bit mute on that," said Jack. "But there were rumors around the station that the detective in charge accidentally touched the body without gloves on, so the coroner was forced to rule out any DNA evidence. It's a rookie mistake, but does happen."

"What items were with the body when the cops arrived?" asked Greg.

"Uh, there was a purse with a wallet, keys, ChapStick, jewelry…that's about it."

"Was there a camera, or a phone, there?" I asked.

"No," replied Jack. "No phone or camera of any kind."

"That's odd," I said. "You said Rachel mentioned a camera."

"Anything else?" said Jack.

"No, thanks," replied Greg. He hung up.

Rachel sat beside us unusually quiet. I could only imagine what she thought about us talking about her as though she wasn't there. "I'm sorry…" I began.

"Don't be," said Rachel. "Who'd believe that you had a ghost among you? The thing is, I remember having a camera with me."

A thought struck me. "Does your phone have a camera?"

"Yeah," said Rachel.

"That's the camera," I said. "Don't you see? We were thinking that you had a camcorder, but in reality, the camera was your phone. Every cell phone has a built in camera these days and they have remarkable picture quality."

"And I always had my phone with me," said Rachel. "It should have been discovered with my body. Unless…"

"Unless what?" asked Jackie.

"Now I remember," said Rachel with excitement. "I hid my phone. That's right. I recorded something on my phone. I don't remember what, yet, but I went to the computer lab to make copies of what I filmed so that I could send it to different law enforcement agencies. But, I never got the chance. When I reached the lab, I heard footsteps coming after me, so I hid my phone. It's under the filing cabinet by the window."

"We should go look," I suggested.

"Problem," said Jackie. "It's been a year. What if the janitor found it and threw it away? The likelihood of it still being there is very slim."

"But what if it is there?" I said. "We have to try."

"Does anyone else find it odd?"

We all looked at Greg.

"Detective Reiss was the detective in charge of the case," said Greg. "He has been a detective for over twenty years. Why would he make such a rookie mistake of touching the body without gloves? He had to have known that such a move would make any DNA evidence found inadmissible in court."

"We all make mistakes sometimes," said Jackie.

"I don't think so," said Greg.

"You realize what you're implying," I said.

"Yes," replied Greg.

"I don't want to go down this road," I said. "Let's look for the phone first, and if it's there it may shed some light on all this, and perhaps it will jog Rachel's memory."

"You're right," said Greg. "Let's go."

"I'll go," I said, "with Rachel. If we all troop down there, it might look suspicious. Remember, the murderer is still out there."

Chapter 7

I snatched my keys and purse and ran off to the college. Within fifteen minutes, I was hoofing it toward the computer lab building. I ran inside and headed straight for the lab. I breathed a sigh of relief to find it empty. I didn't want anyone to know why I was there, nor did I want to explain myself.

I spotted the filing cabinet in the far corner under the window. Wasting no time, I darted toward it, dropping to my knees. Sweat beaded on my back as I wiggled it from the wall a bit so that I could feel behind it.

"Anything?" said Rachel.

I continued to feel around under the cabinet. Frustration creased my brow as I found nothing. I was about to give up when I felt a lump under the carpet. Quickly,

I pulled it up just enough to reveal a small flip phone. I snatched it.

"Lose something?"

I cursed silently at being caught. Slowly, I stood up, shoving the phone in my pocket, hoping that no one noticed. Professor Vincent stood behind me.

"Contact lens," I said, even though I didn't wear them.

He nodded in affirmation. "Hope you found it."

I looked around the empty room, wishing that there were more people. I felt very uncomfortable with Professor Vincent here, and a bit trapped. "I wouldn't worry about it," I said, making a move to leave.

Professor Vincent cut me off. "What's the hurry?"

"I really need to leave," I said.

Professor Vincent cornered me against the filing cabinet, placing both arms on each side of me. "There's no hurry," he said. He glanced down my shirt.

"Professor," I said, "I have to go. Now, please leave me alone."

"Please," he said. "You don't mean that. You know you are a very beautiful woman. Very hot blooded, I'm sure. I love that."

He leaned in for a kiss. I placed my hands on his chest and pushed him away with all my strength.

"A little spit fire," said Professor Vincent, charging for me again.

A scraping sound filled the room as a metal basket with papers in it flew across the cabinet. It struck Professor Vincent in the head. Stunned, he cradled his forehead a moment, staring at me in disbelief. I was too far away to have touched it, and he knew it. Rachel appeared and kicked the man in the knee caps. He fell to the ground, groaning. Hurriedly, I bolted from the room and left the building.

"What a creep," said Rachel. "I knew I never liked him. How did he get to be a professor?"

"I don't know," I said, wanting to get as far away as I could.

"You should report him," said Rachel.

"And who would believe me?" I said. "It's my word against his and he has tenure. And it's not like I can use you as a witness."

"Good point."

I went back to my apartment and locked the door once I got in. I waved the phone at Jackie and Greg. They both beamed. I found my laptop and turned it on. While I waited for it to boot up, I relayed to them what happened with Professor Vincent.

"That bastard," said Greg. "You should have let me come with you."

"Doesn't matter right now," I said. "Rachel took care of it. Unfortunately, I still have to take his class."

My computer had finally finished booting up. I took the memory card out of Rachel's phone and placed it in the card reader on my laptop. Instantly, a file opened. We watched in horror at the video that played on my monitor.

Professor Vincent and a woman appeared on the screen. The two struggled violently. Vincent slapped her across the face, sending her flying to the ground. He proceeded to violate her in a manor I do not wish to describe. Let's just say he ripped off her clothes and lay on top her. Afterward, he zipped up his pants. The woman lay unmoving. She was clearly very hurt.

Then, another guy appeared.

"That's Detective Reiss," said Greg.

Reiss and Vincent argued and shoved each other around a bit. Later, Vincent stormed off, but Reiss remained. The man pulled something out of his pocket. The way he held it told me it was a needle. He bent down and injected the woman with something. Then, he turned and noticed Rachel with the camera. After that, the screen went blank.

We all sat in stunned silence.

"Now I know who killed me," said Rachel.

"I think we're all in deep shit," I said, stating the obvious. Everyone agreed.

Chapter 8

We sat around the computer, wondering what to do next. Now I knew why Rachel didn't run off to the police right away. Yet, I also knew that we couldn't keep this.

"We need to go to the cops," I said.

"Are you crazy?" yelled Greg. "That was a cop that killed that girl."

"I know," I said, "but we can't keep this video. We need to tell someone in authority. With this video that detective will go straight to jail."

"Didn't you mention a detective that thought the entire case was handled poorly?" asked Jackie.

"Yeah, Detective Shorts," replied Greg. "He was the only one on the force that was outspoken about the entire affair. He pursued the investigation on his own for a bit, but without any more evidence, he had to let it go."

"Well, I think we have the evidence he needs," I said. "We should give him a call."

Before we could do anything the screech of tires peeled the air. Greg glanced out the window. "That's my car!" he yelled and tore out of the apartment.

His heavy boots pounded the floor in the hallway as he ran to the parking lot. Jackie followed after him, leaving the door wide open.

I took the memory card out of my computer and held it in my palm. A noise out in the hall caught my attention.

"Jackie?" I poked my head out.

Without warning, a great weight crashed into me, knocking me to the floor. A hand reached for the memory card that had flown out of my hand. I lunged for it. A sharp smack across my cheek sent me flying again. I gasped as a steel toed shoe rammed into my stomach. The assailant snatched the memory card and dashed out the door. I heard his footsteps fade as he disappeared.

"Mel!" Jackie leaned over me. She and Greg helped me up.

I breathed deeply several times to get my breath back. "He took the card," I said.

Greg pulled out his phone and called the cops. He and Jackie helped me to the couch.

"What happened?" asked Rachel reappearing.

"Where were you?" demanded Greg.

"I went after the car," said Rachel, "but I lost the thief."

"You should have stayed here," scolded Greg, "Someone attacked Mel and took the memory card with our only evidence of your murder. Because of you—"

"Stop," I interrupted. "It's not her fault. Rachel, you might want to leave. The cops will be here soon."

Rachel nodded in understanding and vanished.

A knock sounded at the door. The cops had arrived rather quickly. "You called about a break-in," said a guy in uniform.

"Yes," said Greg.

"Excuse me," said a man in a suit. He was tall with a well-defined body shape. The man obviously worked out. "Detective Shorts," he said, introducing himself. "I'll handle this," he said to the guys in uniform. He walked over to me and inspected the bruise forming on my cheek. "Name?"

"Mellow Summers, but everyone calls me Mel," I replied.

"Do you need a paramedic?" he asked.

"I'll be okay," I said.

"Mickey," he called a female officer over, "take pictures of her bruises. I'm sorry, ma'am, but we have to for evidence when we catch the intruder."

I sat still and allowed Mickey to take pictures of my cheek and my stomach. I had more bruises than I originally thought.

"Now," said Detective Shorts, "Tell me what happened."

We relayed how someone had stolen Greg's car, for which the police put an APB on. I explained that Jackie and Greg ran out to the parking lot to chase the car thief, leaving me alone in the apartment. Afterward, I gave a detailed account of the guy that broke in and knocked me around before leaving.

"Can you describe him?" asked the detective.

"No," I said. "He was dressed in black and wore a ski mask."

"Height?"

"About yours."

"Build?"

I thought a moment. "I'd say about average build. He was strong, but like I said, with the mask, I didn't get a good look at him. It happened so quickly."

"Did he take anything?"

"The memory card." The words were out of my mouth before I had a chance to stop it.

"Memory card?" quizzed Detective Shorts.

"Yes, that's what the guy took," I said.

"Seems odd," said the detective. "Most thieves go for jewels or things of value. Why would he take a memory card?"

"I don't know," I replied and glared at Jackie and Greg to remain silent. "I never got a chance to look at it."

"Where did you get this memory card?"

"I found it on campus in the computer lab," I said.

"By itself?"

I figured there would be no fooling the detective, but I didn't want to tell him what was on the card because without it, how could I prove it? "I was at the computer lab on campus," I said, "when I had to get something from the filing cabinet there. That's when I noticed something sticking out of the carpet behind it. I picked it up and it was a phone. The phone was dead so I figured the memory card within it would tell me whose it was. So I brought it here to plug it into my laptop."

"You have a laptop and you were at the computer lab on campus," said the detective.

"Yeah, I needed to email someone and we don't have the internet hooked up yet; and I don't like carting my computer around," I replied. It was true enough. I hated taking my laptop out of the apartment and we hadn't gotten the internet hooked up. Detective Shorts seemed to have bought the story.

"You had a break-in before haven't you?" asked Detective Shorts.

"Yes," replied Jackie, "we came home soon after moving in and there was stuff everywhere."

The detective made notes in his notepad. His expression remained unreadable. "All right, Miss Summers, we'll put an APB on the car and put a description out on the intruder. However, since you can't give me many details we may not catch him. I can have a patrol car drive by here for the next few days. If you remember anything, don't hesitate to give me a call." He handed me his card.

The police left after they finished taking pictures and dusting for prints. I knew they'd never find the guy. He was a professional who wanted only the memory card.

"I guess we're at square one," said Rachel, appearing from thin air. Greg and Jackie both jumped. Being used to her comings and goings, I barely noticed her.

"Not quite" I said. "We now know who killed you. We just need to prove it."

"How do you propose to do that?" asked Greg.

"We'll just have to follow Detective Reiss and Professor Vincent. I'd like to know what the connection is between the two," I replied.

"Are you crazy?"

I looked at Greg. He thought I was nuts. Perhaps I was. "Look," I said, "we have to do something. Those two have gotten away with murder and rape. I want to know how they know each and what they are involved in. We'll have to have cameras with us at all times and if we can get something, then we'll take it to Detective Shorts."

"And what if he's crooked?" asked Jackie.

"There has to be at least one honest cop in this town," I said.

"How are we going to follow them and stay on top of our responsibilities?" asked Greg.

"We have a ghost," I said. "Rachel, do you think you can keep tabs on them?"

"Certainly." Rachel jumped at the chance.

"Follow their movements and find out their routine," I said. "And if we're lucky, we might be able to catch them on something."

Jackie filled my shift the next couple of days at the Candle Shoppe so that I could take it easy. I appreciated it. Greg stopped by often to check up on me. I thought it was really sweet.

When I finally went back to work, I was glad to find that nothing had changed. The Candle Shoppe was not busy, which didn't bother me. I busied myself, restocking some shelves and arranging the displays. The bell above the door rang and in walked Greg.

"For you," he said, handing me a red rose.

I took the flower. It smelled wonderful. I gave him a hug.

The bell above the door rang again. Seven guys walked in all dressed in leather. I recognized them immediately as the bikers that I had stood up to at Zappy's. My blood started pounding.

"You," said the tall guy whose nose I had broken. "You broke my nose."

"That was a while ago," I said, "and you deserved it." I could have kicked myself for that remark. Was I trying to get myself killed?

"Not many people stand up to me," said the guy, "but you did. You got guts. I like that. My name's Tiny." He held out his hand.

I stared at him. Tiny? He was anything but tiny. I took his hand not wanting to offend him. "Mel," I said, introducing myself.

"Well, Mel, I came down to apologize for my behavior," said Tiny. "I normally don't act like that. It took guts to do what you did. You now have a friend in this town."

I wasn't sure if I was grateful or frightened. I certainly was not trying to make friends when I broke Tiny's nose.

Tiny noticed the fading bruise on my cheek. "Someone hit you? Did you beat her?" he turned on Greg. Tiny picked him up as though he weighed nothing.

"No, please," I pleaded. "He didn't do anything. Someone broke into my apartment when I was home a few days back. He was nowhere around when it happened. And I'd appreciate it if you didn't mangle my boyfriend."

Tiny eyed me a bit before putting Greg down. "You should take better care of your woman. Who was it?"

"Unfortunately, the guy was all in black and wore a

ski mask," I said. "The cops said they'd put a description out, but were less than hopeful about catching the guy."

"The cops are useless," said Tiny. "Hey, Sombrero"—a really tanned guy with tattoos all over his arms stepped forward—"put the word out. Anyone know anything about a break-in at Mel's is to tell us right away."

Sombrero left to carry out his orders.

"I don't like people messing with my friends," said Tiny. "We'll find the guy. He'll never bother you again."

"Thanks," I said. I didn't want to know what Tiny had in mind.

"What's going on here?" Mr. Stilton came out of his office. He looked at all of us. I had no way of explaining seven bikers in the shop. Fortunately, I didn't have to.

"We're here to buy some stuff," said Tiny. He snatched the first thing closest to him. It turned out to be a heart shaped basket with romantic candles and perfume all tied with red and pink ribbons. It didn't go with his leather, spikes, and tattoos.

I covered my mouth to keep from laughing. The others followed suit, each snatching the closest thing off a shelf. They went to the counter and I rang up the purchases. Mr. Stilton watched as I took their money and put it in the cash register.

"Let's roll, boys," said Tiny as they all left.

"I better go," said Greg, giving me a peck on the cheek.

I went back to rearranging the displays when Mr. Stilton walked up behind me.

"You okay?" he asked.

"Yeah," I said, "Why wouldn't I be?"

"I heard about the break-in," he said. He took the big, round candles out of my hands. "Take the rest of the day off," he said, "I can handle the store. Fridays are usually slow around here."

I thanked my boss and grabbed my things. Greg met me outside, holding all the stuff that Tiny and his friends had bought. "What..." I began.

"Tiny gave me all this and told me to take you out for a very romantic evening," said Greg, answering my unspoken question.

The roar of motorcycles grabbed my attention. I glanced over and saw Tiny and his pals. He winked at me as they rode down the street.

"Of all the people to make friends with," said Greg, "you just had to befriend the only biker gang in this town."

"I didn't mean to," I said, weakly.

"Don't sweat it," replied Greg. "It could prove useful."

I kissed Greg good-bye and told him I'd meet up with him later. I decided to grab my camcorder from my car and go back to the college. I had a video assignment to do and wanted to get some filming in. My topic: college student life.

I stood just outside the student center with my camera going. After interviewing a bunch of other people eating their lunch, or just relaxing, I figured I had enough to do something with it. I knew this wasn't Oscar winning material, but it would do for my class assignment. I just hoped that Professor Vincent would forget about the incident in the computer lab.

And speaking of Professor Vincent, I noticed him pop up on the LCD screen of my camera. Curiosity got the better of me. I zoomed in. He fidgeted as he stood in a secluded corner. His manner told me that something wasn't right. He clearly did not want to be seen, or bothered, and he was obviously waiting for someone.

Detective Reiss walked into my screen. Intrigued, I zoomed in even more. What were they up to? The two talked a bit and then exchanged brown packages. I had watched enough CSI and detective shows to know that this couldn't be good. I continued filming their exchange. It only lasted a couple of minutes before both parted and went separate ways. Odd, I thought.

My gut told me that they were up to no good. I pulled out my cell and called Greg. He answered on the first ring. "Greg," I said, "I need you to distract Professor Vincent."

"What?"

"I just filmed him and that Detective Reiss exchange something. Vincent is headed back to his office now. I need you to get him out of it so I can search it."

"Are you crazy?"

"Do you want to know what he's up to or not?"

"Okay, okay," relented Greg. "Give me a moment."

I dashed into the building that housed all of the teacher's offices. Thankfully, there was a ladies' room right outside Professor Vincent's office. I waited near there. Greg showed up a few minutes later.

"You want to tell me what this is about?" he asked.

"Haven't time," I replied. "I just witnessed him and

Reiss exchange packages. Vincent took it into his office just now. If I can get a look at it, we might be able to find out what those two are doing."

Greg sighed, but agreed that it might work. He went into Vincent's office. I listened just outside the door as the two talked. Greg pretended to have a problem with the assignment and wanted Vincent to follow him out-side. Despite his pleas, the professor refused to bite. Frustrated, I knew that if he didn't leave the office soon, I would miss my window of opportunity. I spotted a fire alarm and figured it was now or never. I pulled it and ran to the ladies' room.

Instantly, the hall filled with people evacuating their offices and heading for the exit. I peeked out the door, waiting for the hallway to empty. I watched as Professor Vincent and Greg left.

I slipped out and pretended to go with the crowd, hanging back a bit. When I reached the office door, I took a quick survey to make certain no one saw me. The door was unlocked. I snuck in, closing it behind me. I only had minutes and headed straight for the desk.

Drawers opened and closed as I searched for the package. I hoped he didn't have time to hide it some-place. I found a drawer that refused to budge. Locked. It had to be the one. Sirens echoed in the distance coming nearer. I gritted my teeth and ripped a bobby pin from my hair. I silently thanked Jackie for teaching me how to pick a lock as I put the pin in the key hole. Click. I pulled the drawer out.

Within sat bags of white powdery stuff. I knew they

had to be drugs. I found the brown package he had carried earlier. Quickly, I opened it to reveal more. I opened one and tasted it. Drugs all right.

The sirens stopped right outside the building. Shoot! I took out my camera and turned it on. Hurriedly, I snapped pictures of the stuff and slammed the drawer shut. I ran out of the office. Heavy boots sounded in the stairwell. I darted into the ladies' room again. They searched the offices at the far end first. When no one was looking, I seized my chance and dashed to the other exit, hoping no one was there. I ran down the stairs and out the door into the sunlight, slipping in among those gathered around the scene.

I pretended to be just as curious as everyone else as the firemen did their job. After a few minutes, the fire chief declared it a false alarm and allowed people to go back inside. I followed the rest of the crowd as it dispersed, staying clear of Professor Vincent. I went back to the student center and found Greg waiting for me.

"Did you get it?" he asked.

I pulled out my camera and showed him the pictures I took.

"This is great," said Greg. "Now we can take it to the cops."

"And say what, exactly? That I broke into his office and illegally got this? I want more evidence. So far, all I've got is assumptions and circumstantial stuff."

"You sound like a regular lawyer," said Greg.

"Think about it," I said. "We may be able to get Vincent on possession of drugs, but Reiss can still deny everything. He can claim anything was in that bag. Besides, I want them for Rachel's murder."

"You're taking this personally," said Greg.

"Well, yeah," I replied. "They got away with two deaths."

Greg put his hand on my shoulder. "You are a unique person," he said. "Just don't do anything to get yourself killed."

I kissed him good-bye and ran off. The drive back home was quick and uneventful. I dumped my stuff on the couch when I got back in the apartment. Putting my sleuthing on hold, I settled down to do my homework.

The homework went rather quickly, despite being boring. A few essays to write, one film edited. I especially took out the bit with Reiss and Vincent. except, this time, I made a backup copy of it. It was dark by the time I finished my schoolwork.

I stretched my muscles. At least now I'd have the weekend to relax. Jackie and I managed to get the entire weekend off. She walked through the door moments later.

"Where were you?" I asked her.

"Oh, here and there," she said. "I decided to go for a bit of a drive and explore the surrounding area. How was your day?"

I reiterated my capturing of Reiss and Vincent on my camera. Jackie gasped when I told her about sneaking into Professor Vincent's office and what I found. "We need to find what that Detective Reiss is up to," I said.

"I guess we could follow him," said Jackie.

"That's an idea."

"Hey," said Jackie, "I just remembered. Tomorrow the police station is having an open house. They didn't call it that, but as part of their public relations they are doing tours. We could go and somehow slip away."

I smiled at Jackie. "Look at you. You're turning into a regular Nancy Drew. But how are we going to sneak around without getting caught?"

"Your boyfriend has a cousin that works there," replied Jackie.

I had to hand it to her. She did think this out. Maybe it would work.

Chapter 9

The next morning we went straight down to the police station for the public tours. Greg told us that he had talked to Jack. Jack agreed to meet us down there. Greg had wanted to come, but I turned him down. Jackie and I together would have enough difficulty sneaking around. A third person would be even more conspicuous.

A huge crowd had gathered for the tours. Secretly, I was pleased. The more people, the better we can slip away. We got in line and waited our turn to be allowed in. It finally came. We found ourselves bustled in with a group of people. A nice young lady in a black skirt suit led us into the main lobby. "Here is where members of the public enter and wait to speak with the next available officer," she said. I ignored her.

"Look around for Jack," I said.

"We don't even know what he looks like," said Jackie.

She was right. We hadn't thought about that part of the plan. We hung toward the back of the crowd, hoping that Jack would find us. A hand grasped my and Jackie's shoulders. We turned around to be met by a man putting a finger over his mouth, signaling silence. He pulled us around a corner and away from the rest of the crowd.

"Jack," I said.

He nodded. Jack wore black rimmed glasses and had on slacks and a button up shirt. "I hope you two know what you're doing," he said.

"Just take us to where Detective Reiss is," I told him.

"All right," Jack replied, "but be careful. They found out about my hacking into that file. They don't know it's me, but everyone is on high alert."

Jack led us through the building on many twists and turns. I quickly became confused. I hoped I wasn't going to have to try and find a way out. Jack took us to a secluded part of the building. "Here," he said. "Reiss' office is here. Just don't get caught."

A noise sounded in the distance. Jack ran off to check it out, muttering something about staying put. Jackie and I didn't listen. I watched Detective Reiss, intently. He fiddled around in his office. Someone ran in, gave him a message, and left. Reiss glanced at the piece of paper, crumpled it, and put it in the garbage. He left his office.

I motioned to Jackie to follow. We tip toed down the hall after Reiss, trying our best to be quiet. We stayed a distance away so as not to attract attention. We squeezed against a wall in the shadows when he turned around. He didn't want to be followed.

Jackie and I continued after him. He went down some stairs and into the basement. We went after him. He passed through another door and I caught it before it could close. Jackie and I slipped through. I pulled her behind some crates. Reiss stopped at a desk. He talked with the guy behind the counter, but I couldn't hear what he said.

The guy behind the counter pressed a buzzer, allowing Reiss through. He went in. Jackie and I waited. Neither of us talked for fear of giving ourselves away. After a couple of minutes, Reiss came out the door, holding something. I noticed he shoved it in his pockets when the guy at the counter looked at him. He filled out some form and then headed back to the door.

I bolted for the door and once again caught it before it closed. Jackie and I stepped into the stairwell. Reiss had already made it to the first floor. Jackie and I trailed after him. We took the stairs two at a time, being careful not to make any noise. We went through the door only pausing long enough to check that we hadn't been noticed.

Reiss was nowhere to be seen. "Where'd he go?" I whispered.

Jackie shrugged her shoulder in response.

I motioned for Jackie to follow. We crept through the hallway. I searched in rooms, but found no sign of Detective Reiss. My mind raced, trying to discover what happened to him and wondering if we should go back to the lobby. I had almost reached a decision when—

"What are you doing here," demanded a gruff voice.

Jackie and I whirled around. Detective Reiss stood before me and he looked angry. I immediately disliked the guy.

"We were on the tour," I began, "and we got lost searching for the restroom."

"Why were you following me?"

My heart skipped a beat. I pinched Jackie to remind her to stay silent. I hoped he didn't see me. "Following you?" I tried to sound incredulous, hoping my voice didn't give away the truth. "We were not following you."

"Really," growled Detective Reiss.

I had the sudden impulse to run. Only my resolve kept me from acting on it.

"There you two are." Jack marched down the corridor towards us. "I've been looking everywhere for you two. Don't you know you are supposed to stay near the tour group and not wander? Come with me."

"These two are with you?" asked Detective Reiss.

"Of course they are," replied Jack. "I've been searching for them everywhere."

The expression on Reiss' face told me he didn't buy it.

"I apologize if they caused you any inconvenience, Detective," said Jack. "Now, if you'll excuse me. I have a tour to run." He motioned for us to follow. Jackie and I didn't argue, grateful to be out of there.

"What did you two think you were doing?" hissed Jack. "You should have waited for me."

"I'm sorry," I said, "but you disappeared and I didn't want to lose a chance to follow Detective Reiss."

"What did you find out?" asked Jack.

"He went to the basement," said Jackie, "and took something from there."

"The evidence locker is down there," said Jack. "We've had problems of things missing from there. And it's strange that Reiss would be down there since he hasn't arrested anyone lately."

"Do you think he's stealing from the evidence locker?" I asked.

"That's quite an accusation," said Jack, "but I guess it's possible."

We had reached the entrance to the building. I thanked Jack and we left. Jackie and I went back to our apartment. We had nothing else to do that day and I wanted to get ahead on my school work.

Rachel popped in as had become her habit. "Vincent doesn't do much that can be considered illegal," she said. "He hits on just about every young female he finds, but otherwise, he didn't do anything worth calling the cops."

"I found some drugs in his office," I said.

"Really?"

"Yeah, but I want to get him and that detective on more than just possession."

"That detective likes to frequent a place on the outskirts of town," said Rachel. "It's called Sal's. It's a strip joint."

"I guess I know where I'm going tonight," I said, "When does he go there?"

"About every night at midnight," said Rachel.

Chapter 10

I dressed in a rather revealing outfit for my trip to Sal's. I had to borrow some of Jackie's clothes. It was a good thing we wore the same size. According to Rachel, you got into Sal's if you showed a little skin. Despite my discomfort, I justified that it was necessary to find out what Reiss was up to.

I was at Sal's within the hour. It was about fifteen miles outside of town. A perfect place for a bar that offered exotic dancing. I parked the car and got out.

The man at the door took one look at me and let me in. I flirted a bit with him like the other girls did. Blend in, I told myself. Once again, loud music bombarded me. I hated loud music. I wandered around the place. Women danced on the stage around poles. They wore enough to barely cover the essentials.

The full service section seemed to be in the back, which was guarded by a couple of muscular bouncers. I had no desire to get on a first name basis with them. The bartender bustled about the bar, filling orders. Men and women filled the place. I guess some people didn't care where they got drunk.

I walked over to the bar and ordered a Morgan Coke. Everyone else had a drink; I figured I should too to avoid arousing suspicion. I accepted the drink graciously and continued my wandering. No sign of Detective Reiss. I glanced at my watch. Half past midnight. According to Rachel, he should have been here for half an hour already.

"Where is he?" I asked Rachel.

"I don't know. He should be here," said Rachel.

We split up. Rachel searched the VIP section, while I meandered around the main floor. Still no sign of him.

"Hey!" yelled Rachel, getting my attention. She waved me over. "He's in here."

I peeked through the curtain she held out. Detective Reiss sat in the room on a cushy chair. His unbuttoned shirt showed off his hairy chest. He seemed to be enjoying the pleasure of the woman giving him a lap dance. "Nice to know what those who swear to protect and serve do in their down time," I whispered.

"Yeah, he's really broken up," said Rachel.

I spotted an untouched shot of tequila. "Distract the bouncer," I told Rachel. She vanished. I peered over at the bouncer who suddenly seemed be bothered by an unseen assailant. Chuckling to myself, I drank the tequila and stumbled into the private room.

I tripped over my own feet and wobbled, pretending to be drunk. "What's all the fuss in here?" I slurred. I hoped my performance was convincing.

Everyone stared at me. I stumbled around some more until I practically fell into Reiss' lap. "I know you," I said. "You're that guy that handled that dead girl's murder."

"Someone get rid of her please," said Detective Reiss.

"Yeah, it was you all right," I continued. "Some think you didn't handle it right, but that's not true is it?" I leaned in close, letting my alcohol breath overwhelm him. "It's good to know you're doing so well. especially since, you're the one that killed Rachel."

Detective Reiss stared at me. I studied his features for any sign of recognition at her name. His brow flickered for just a moment before he controlled himself. "I think you've had too much to drink," he said.

"That I have," I blurted. "You think you got away with it, but it's only a matter of time until some piece of evidence shows up. He killed her!" I twirled in a circle to make my drunk act appear complete. In hindsight, I might have overdone it. I also hadn't thought it all the way through.

Detective Reiss stood up and approached me. Instantly, I knew I had to get out of there. I edged toward the exit.

"What's your hurry?" said Reiss. "You look like a reasonable girl. And the fun is just starting." His eyes wandered up and down my body. I knew he undressed me with them. I inched closer to the exit.

Reiss lunged and grabbed my arm tightly. His grip told me that I was going nowhere.

"There you are," said a female voice as a woman in tight leather burst into the room. "I've been looking everywhere for you." She noticed Reiss' grip on my arm. "Hey, pal, get your hands off my woman."

Reiss reluctantly let go. "You might want to keep a better eye on your girlfriend."

"That's between me and her," said the woman, waving her curly blonde locks. "Come on, babe," she said to me.

I didn't argue.

"Take your slut and stay out of here," said Reiss. "And remind her to keep her mouth shut, before someone shuts it for her."

I had had it. I could take a few insults, but calling me a slut was the last straw. I don' know why I did it; if it was the alcohol, or Rachel's influence. I whirled around, raised my fist, and plowed it right into Reiss' nose. I felt the bones break and warm blood ooze over my fist.

The woman who saved me stared at me in shock. She seized my wrist and hauled me to the doorway. We found it blocked by a bouncer.

"Let us through," she said, "or you can explain to Tiny why we're late."

That had the desired effect. Tiny must have had quite a reputation. The man scooted away from the door and we entered the main part of the bar.

We remained silent as the woman pulled me through the building and to another secluded room. Inside, sat Tiny and his pals, plus a few women. These girls were all dressed in tight leather and knee high boots. No strippers were present.

"I got her," said the woman. She released my wrist and planted a huge kiss on Tiny's lips.

"Mel," said Tiny, "meet my girl Elise. I noticed you go into the cop's room so I sent her in to get you out."

"Thanks," I said.

"I didn't know you liked these places," Tiny said.

"I don't," I replied. "I was following someone."

One of Tiny's pals gave me a seat. "Explain," said Tiny.

I took a deep breath. "You all know that girl Rachel that was murdered last year."

They nodded in affirmation.

"I know who killed her. It was Detective Reiss. I had evidence that connected him to her murder, but before I could get it to the cops, someone broke into my place and stole it. I found out that he likes to hang out here, so I followed him. I was hoping that I could somehow get him to screw up and pin him for her murder."

"So that's why you went in there," said Elise. "Girl, you've watched too many cop dramas."

"Well, I might not have thought it all the way through," I admitted.

"You certain he did it?" asked Tiny.

"I know he did," I replied.

Just then, Rachel showed up. Leave it to her to just appear when it was inconvenient. "What happened to you?" she demanded.

"Rachel," I replied, "where were you? I could have used you in there! And you've got to quit popping in without warning. I mean really—" I stopped speaking when I realized everyone stared at me as though I had lost my mind. "Did I happen to mention that I can talk to ghosts?"

"I think you had one too many," said Elise, grabbing some water.

Knowing where this was headed, Rachel picked up a bottle of beer and handed it to Tiny. Everyone watched in awe as the bottle appeared to be moving by itself.

"Here you go," said Rachel as she handed him the beer.

Tiny jumped a bit. "You're for real," he said. "My Nana was like you. Said she could see things that no one else could."

"Is that Rachel?" asked one of Tiny's friends.

"Yes," I replied. "She showed up and told me who killed her. She even helped me find the missing proof, but someone else must have known about it too."

"I hate cops," said Tiny, "but I especially hate dirty cops. That Reiss character comes in here all the time for a lap dance and something more. No one goes in there. Being a cop he can make anyone's life hell."

"How do you plan to prove his guilt?" asked Elise.

"I was hoping to shock him into a confession." After I spoke, I realized how stupid my words sounded. As a seasoned detective, he'd never fall for that. "I know it sounds dumb, but at this point, the only way to convict him is to get a confession."

"You're probably right," said Tiny. "Unfortunately, that might be difficult."

"That guy burns me up," said Sombrero. "Always has something weird going on."

"He steals stuff from the evidence locker at the

station," I said. "I saw him do it. My guess is drugs. I caught him and a college professor exchanging packages. And I found drugs in the professor's office."

Tiny raised his eyebrows. "What'd you do? Break in?"

My face reddened in embarrassment. In my attempt to prove someone's guilt for murder, I ended up breaking a few laws myself. "Yeah," I said. "And I snuck into the police station and followed Reiss around."

Tiny roared with laughter. "You got guts!"

"Who's the professor?" asked Elise.

"Vincent," I replied, "The guy's a creep. He tried to force himself on me a couple of times."

I heard knuckles crack. Tiny's face contorted in anger. He meant it when he said no one messed with his friends. "Oh, he did? Boys, I think it's time we go to school and get some education."

Tiny's friends all smiled. They understood what he meant. I did too, though I didn't want to know about it.

"Here," Tiny tossed me an onion. "I think it's time you head home. This ain't your kind of party. And the cop will be here for a while."

I thanked everyone and left the building. Despite the cold night air, I relished it. It felt wonderful to get out of that stifling black hole. I breathed deeply, absorbing the fresh air.

I quickly found my car and pulled out onto the highway. Time to head home and to bed. I kept my speed under the limit and made certain not to swerve. I only had the one shot, but I didn't want to get pulled over, regardless. Unfortunately, life had another plan.

Flashing red and blue lights appeared in my rear view mirror. Oh no, I thought. A siren sounded, telling me that I was the one the cop was after. Mumbling a few choice words under my breath, I pulled to the side of the road.

"Quick!" said Rachel. "Eat the onion."

"What?" I said.

Rachel shoved the onion in my mouth, forcing me to take a bite out of it. I practically choked as I chewed and swallowed it. Rachel tossed the onion under the seat.

A tap sounded on my window. I rolled it down. "May I help you, officer?" I asked.

The patrolman pulled back a bit after getting a whiff of my onion breath. Did anyone really think eating an onion would fool the cops?

Another officer appeared at the passenger side window. He shined a light inside. A feeling of dread encompassed me.

"Ma'am, you mind telling me where you are headed?" said the officer by my window.

"Home," I replied. "Don't you want my license and registration?" I thought their manner was odd. Usually, when you get a ticket they asked to see your registration, insurance, and license.

"Please step out of the car," said the cop.

"Why?" I asked.

"Ma'am, please step out of the car," repeated the officer.

I unbuckled my seatbelt and opened the car. "Mind telling me what is going on?" I know you shouldn't get confrontational with a patrolman, but something didn't seem right.

"Put your hands on the car," said the officer.

"Look," I said, "I have a right to know what is going on and why you pulled me over."

"Is this your car?" asked the second officer.

"Yes," I replied.

"You do realize that it was reported stolen," said the first cop.

"That's impossible," I said. "It's my car and I never reported it stolen."

"That remains to be seen," said the first officer.

"Look," I said, "My ID is in the car. The registration and proof of insurance is in the glove compartment. I can prove to you that this is my car."

"Put your hands on the hood of the car," said the first officer.

"Ma'am," said the second cop, "please put your hands on the car, or we'll have to add resisting arrest."

Reluctantly, I put my hands on the car and allowed the officers to handcuff me. Before I knew it, they led me to the patrol car and stuck me in the back. Now I was being arrested for stealing my own car. Something wasn't right and I knew who was responsible for my car being reported stolen.

The officer that had been at my window opened the door to get in. His hat flew off his head and rolled down the road. I knew Rachel had done it. She laughed uncontrollably.

I watched as the guy walked over to pick up his hat. Rachel kicked it and sent it down the road again. Despite my glum mood, I did find it funny.

"Come on!" yelled the second officer,."Just grab your hat and let's go."

Rachel tired of her fun and allowed the man to get his hat. He got in the car and we were off just as another patrol car showed up with a tow truck.

The ride to the police station went quickly. I spent the time wondering what I was going to do. Rachel appeared next to me. "Rachel," I whispered, hoping the cops didn't hear me, "I need you to go back to the apartment. Now isn't the time to be talking to a ghost."

She agreed and vanished.

The car stopped at the station. One of the officers opened the door to the back and hauled me out. There was no way I'd get out by myself with my hands behind my back. The officer placed his hand around my arm and guided me into the building. The station suddenly lost all its charm now that I was being brought in on suspicion of being a car thief.

The officer led me through the lobby. I filled out paperwork and they took my prints. They also took my picture. The vain side of me hoped I looked good. Stupid, I know. After about twenty minutes of being booked, I was led to an interrogation room.

"Don't I get a phone call?" I asked the officer taking me to the room.

He grunted in response.

"Miss Summers." I turned toward the voice. Detective Reiss smiled at me. It was not one of those nice to see you grins.

"No!" I yelled, pulling away. "I don't want to be questioned by him!"

The officer holding my arm resisted my struggles, pulling me into the room.

"No!" I screamed. "Not him! I'll talk to anyone, but him." I twisted and turned, trying to get away. I know it didn't help my image, but I had a bad feeling about all of this. "Let me go!"

"Miss Summers, please calm down," said Detective Reiss.

"I won't let you question me!" I twisted some more. Finally, two officers pinned me against the wall.

"What's going on here?" Detective Shorts arrived. He looked at me, Reiss, and the other two cops.

"I don't want to be interrogated by him," I repeated.

"Let her go," Detective Shorts told the officers holding me down. "Now, tell me what is going on."

"She was arrested for car theft," said Detective Reiss. "Had a few drinks at Sal's and is now resisting arrest."

"Bullshit!" I yelled. "It's my car and I can prove it, but the cops that arrested me never gave me a chance. And I never told you I was at Sal's."

"I learned it from the arresting officer," said Reiss.

"The hell you did," I spat. "I didn't tell them either. But you were at Sal's and threatened me there."

"She's clearly drunk," said Detective Reiss, "and if you don't mind, I have a job to do."

"Give me the file," said Detective Shorts.

"What?" challenged Detective Reiss.

"Take a look at her," said Detective Shorts. "She clearly is not drunk. And since she is adamant about not being interrogated by you, little will be accomplished if you try it. Add to the list that she has now accused you of threatening her."

"You don't believe—"

"The accusation has been made," said Detective Shorts, "which puts you off the case; and it won't be that hard to find out if you and she had a run in at Sal's."

"That woman broke my nose," said Detective Reiss.

"Thank you," replied Detective Shorts, "for confirming your whereabouts tonight. Leave me the file. You are dismissed. Miss Summers, if you please."

I went into the interrogation room and sat down. Detective Shorts closed the door. He undid my handcuffs and offered me some water. I wasn't thirsty. I surveyed my surroundings while I rubbed my wrists. This is not how I planned to spend my night.

"You want to tell me what is going on?" asked Detective Shorts. He pulled out a chair and sat down. "Like, what was that all about?"

"I don't trust that guy."

"Neither do I, but you certainly caused a scene."

"How do you know he isn't listening?" I asked.

"What?"

"I know that's a two way mirror," I said, "and there are cops in the other room listening."

Detective Shorts grinned. "Can't fool you, can I? The intercom is turned off. If anyone is in there, they can't hear us."

I glared at him. He must have read my mind.

"I'm not lying," he said. "Now, what is going on?"

"I didn't steal the car. That car is mine. The registration

and insurance are in the glove compartment under my name. My ID is still in the car in my purse. License plate is 5YGM69."

"Congratulations. Even I don't know my license plate number. This should be easy enough to clear up." Detective Shorts went out of the room for a moment. He came back a minute later. "Now," he said, "tell me the rest of it. Why were you at Sal's? Why did you break Detective Reiss' nose? And, why are you afraid of him?"

I sucked in some air. A part of me wanted to blurt out everything. Another part wanted to remain silent. I didn't know if I could trust the guy in front of me. In the end, I chose to risk it.

"He's a dirty cop," I said.

"That is quite an accusation," said Detective Shorts.

"It's true," I pleaded.

Detective Shorts held up his hand to silence me. He walked over to the camera in the room and unplugged it. "Tell me everything."

Where to begin? "I caught Detective Reiss and Professor Vincent on the university exchanging packages. I wasn't spying. I was actually working on an assignment for my film class and just happened to notice them."

"Did you film the exchange?"

"Yes. I think it was drugs."

"How do know that?"

"I kind of snuck into Professor Vincent's office and found a bunch of drugs in the bottom drawer of his desk."

"You do realize that that is breaking and entering," said Detective Shorts, "and I could arrest you for that."

"My boyfriend did mention that." I slumped in the chair. "Continue."

"Then my friend Jackie and I came to the public tours that were being held here. We snuck off and followed Detective Reiss to the basement. He took something from down there. I didn't see what."

"I'll have to tell Jack to quit doing private tours of the office. I'm well aware that your boyfriend's cousin works in personnel," Detective Shorts finished when he saw my expression. "And then you followed Reiss to Sal's. Want to tell me why you were following him?"

I groaned. This wouldn't be good, but I started talking and now was the time to spill it. "He murdered Rachel," I said. "That girl that was murdered a year ago."

"I know who she is. I also know that Detective Reiss handled that case."

"And he was adamant that Tom did it. But he didn't kill her. I know. I found Rachel's cell phone in the computer lab. I took it home. I know it was hers because the SIM card in the phone said so. She had captured a video on the camera. It showed Reiss and Vincent raping a girl and then killing her. He looked over and saw Rachel. Must have known that she filmed him and killed her.

"When that guy broke into my apartment, he took the memory card from her phone. He killed her. I was following him, hoping to get proof somehow."

After my spiel, Detective Shorts stared at me. I didn't know what he was thinking. He mulled over my statement. "You realize what you just said?"

"Yes."

"If what you say is true, then that means that Detective Reiss not only covered up a crime, but is guilty of theft, and two murders. Except, you don't have the only proof."

"I know," I said. "I wish I did."

"Do you still have the phone?"

"Yes," I said.

Detective Shorts handed me his cell phone. "Call your roommate. Have her bring the phone in. No tricks."

I dialed Jackie's number. "Jackie? Grab Rachel's phone. It's in my nightstand. I need you to bring it to the police station. And bring my camcorder, too. I'll explain later." I knew I had woken her up. At least she was a good sport and didn't ask me any questions. "She's on her way."

A knock sounded at the door. Detective Shorts opened it and talked to the uniformed officer there. I couldn't make out what was said. "Tell me about tonight."

"I followed Reiss to Sal's," I said. "I had a misguided notion of getting him to incriminate himself. He saw me and grabbed my arm." I showed Shorts my arm. He studied the bruises there and made a note. "I broke his nose when he wouldn't let go and called me a slut."

Detective Shorts laughed. "I'm sure he liked that."

Twenty minutes passed and I answered a few more questions. Another knock sounded at the door. Detective Shorts opened it and took a brown paper bag from the uniformed officer. He came back to the table and opened it pulling out Rachel's phone. "Your friend doesn't waste time."

He opened the back of the phone and took out the

SIM card, placing it in his phone. Sure enough, it came up as being registered to Rachel. He put the card back in Rachel's phone.

"I'll take this down to the tech guys as evidence. I'm not going to lie to you, Miss Summers. Reopening the case won't be easy. You made a serious accusation that cannot be proven at this point. You broke into a professor's office, so I'm not sure how I can get a warrant. I'll try. You can file harassment and assault charges against him.

"As for Detective Reiss, I need hard proof of everything you mentioned before I can charge him on anything. He won't bother you about tonight. He was off duty at the time and it would be too much to explain."

"What about a confession," I suggested.

"He's too smart for a wire. And don't get any stupid ideas."

His glare made me glad that he was on my side. "It was a thought," I said, weakly.

"Now, you have a bunch of friends out there, one named Tiny, who are all willing to swear that you were with them tonight. They are also willing to swear that Reiss assaulted you and that it was Tiny who broke his nose. You have interesting friends. And good ones.

"Also, your car checks out. Your ID and registration were in there as you said."

Detective Shorts helped me file harassment charges against Professor Vincent. Afterward, he took out the memory card of my camcorder.

"I suggest you keep a low profile," said Detective Shorts.

"I want to know how my car got reported stolen," I said.

"So do I."

The detective led me to the lobby. He made sure my things were returned and that all charges would be dropped so that nothing appeared on my record. When I left the building, Jackie threw herself at me.

"Mel!" she screamed as she hugged me. "What happened?"

"When you go after something, you don't mess around," said Tiny.

Jackie backed off a little. I hadn't told her about Tiny yet.

"Someone reported my car stolen," I began. "The cops didn't believe my story so they arrested me. Then that Detective Reiss tried to have me brought up on charges of assault against a police officer."

"Bastard," said Tiny.

Jackie drove me home. I knew I'd have to get my car from the impound in the morning. It was already around 4am. Another night lost without sleep.

Chapter 11

After getting my car from the impound lot, which cost me about a hundred bucks, I went straight home. I stayed there with no intention of going out. In fact, I wanted nothing further to do with murder, creepy college professors, cops, bars, loud music, or spying on people. As far as I was concerned, my days as a sleuth were done. Only one problem remained: Rachel.

She spent the weekend badgering me about how I had promised to help her catch her murderer. I understood her frustration, but she didn't seem to understand that I could be seriously injured. I had already been attacked by a college professor, a man whom most people would trust. Now I was probably on the hit list of a detective who only wore the badge so he could hide his illicit activities behind it.

Greg was a darling. He cooked me dinner twice and even served it to me in bed. I had certainly picked a good one for a change. Jackie's eyes burned with jealously at first. She still had trouble finding a reliable boyfriend. Greg smoothed things over when he cooked a meal for all three of us. I relished every minute of it.

Monday came like it always does and with it I had to go to work. Luckily, the Candle Shoppe didn't get any odd customers. Only the regulars came. I was glad for a quiet day. It allowed me a chance to do the Halloween display. I spent the day rearranging shelves in the window. We had a huge assortment of candles for the holiday. I picked through candles shaped like skulls, candy corn, pumpkins, black cats, and ghosts. I laughed at the ghosts. If only people knew that ghosts didn't look like that.

After arranging the candles, scented warmers, and candle stands, I sprinkled Halloween confetti around it. Then, I added some cotton to make it look like everything was wrapped in a spider web. After I had finished, I stepped back to admire my work. Perfect, I thought. Hopefully, people would buy the stuff. Mr. Stilton ordered a bunch of it, which now overflowed in the back storage room.

I glanced out the window like I normally do from time to time. Detective Reiss stood on the other side of the street watching me. An ominous feeling welled in my stomach. He knew that I was aware of his crimes thanks to my stupidly letting him know that.

I backed out of the window, watching him as he

casually strolled down the walk. A sudden awareness that I had painted a target on my back engulfed me. A part of me wished that I had never met Rachel.

The next morning, I got up early to be on time to my film editing class. I found a seat in the back and hoped that Professor Vincent had forgotten about the incident in the computer lab. I shrunk down in my seat when he walked in with other students. Gradually, people filed in and took their seats.

"Welcome class," said Professor Vincent.

I had to hand it to this guy: he was very good at pretending to be normal. I just took notes and pretended to not remember anything from a few days ago.

Professor Vincent droned on and on. I had managed to block out everything as I automatically took notes. Then, it went silent. I looked up. Tiny and his friends stood in the doorway. Oh no, I thought, this could not be good.

Everyone stared as the bikers strolled into the classroom. They each sat in an empty seat. I started packing my stuff.

"Excuse me," said Professor Vincent, "but this is a class and you don't belong here."

"We're your new students," said Tiny.

"Registration ended a month ago," said Vincent.

"Not for us," said Tiny. He glanced around the room. All eyes were on him. "Class is dismissed for the day."

I didn't need telling twice. I grabbed my stuff and headed out the door. Everyone else followed. They read the signs. They knew that a bunch of bikers showing up in class like that was not a good thing. I hung just outside the door to listen.

"What do you want?" demanded Vincent.

Tiny moved dangerously close to the professor. He leaned in letting his bulk intimidate the man. "I know about you and your lust for young women," said Tiny. "Unfortunately for you, you molested one of my friends."

"I don't know what you're talking about," said Vincent. He nervously shoved his papers into his briefcase.

"I think you do." Tiny wrapped his giant hand around Vincent's wrist. "And if I ever hear of you coming near any of the girls here on this college, you just might find yourself on the front of my bike on a long ride outside of town. Got it?"

"You can't threaten me. I'll report you to the police."

"And who do you have as a witness?"

Fear crossed Vincent's brow. He squirmed uncomfortably.

I had seen enough and darted out the door before Tiny and his friends exited the room. There was no point in letting them know that I had overheard the entire proceeding. Tiny meant it when he said he would deal with the creepy professor.

"Mel, did you hear?" Greg ran up to me.

"Hear what?"

"The police got a warrant to search Professor Vincent's office. They're there right now. And they found the packages of drugs that you took pictures of."

"That's great," I said. "So he's going to be arrested?"

"Looks that way," replied Greg. "Detective Shorts is on his way here right now."

Sure enough, Detective Shorts walked down the footpath toward the building I had just exited. He didn't acknowledge me as he passed through the entrance. That was fine by me. The less attention I attracted the better.

Within minutes he came out dragging a handcuffed Professor Vincent. "I'm innocent! I didn't do it! I'll sue all of you!" yelled Vincent loud enough for the residents of a cemetery to hear him.

"Really," growled Detective Shorts. "Tell that to the D.A. when we show him the amount of drugs we found in your office. And don't worry. I have the warrant right here."

"You can't do this," screamed Professor Vincent. "What about those bikers that came here and threatened me?"

"Bikers? I didn't notice any bikers. You got witnesses?" Detective Shorts dragged Professor Vincent down the walk and to the waiting patrol car.

"I guess I don't need to worry about my eight thirty class anymore," I said.

"Hey," said Greg, "you have to come to the party tomorrow night."

"Party?"

"Yeah. Every year they have a Halloween Parade and some of the stores open up for party goers."

"Halloween isn't for another couple of weeks."

"It's the city's way of ensuring that the adults get to have their fun without interfering with Trick or Treaters."

"I've never heard of this before," I said.

"Well the city council voted for it and no one's disputed it. Most figure it gives them a chance to party twice."

"I don't have a costume," I said.

"I'm sure Jackie can help you with that. She's already agreed to come," replied Greg

Figures. Jackie always loved a party. I bet she had already bought a costume for her and for me.

I breezed through the rest of my classes that day. Hardly anything got done. The campus was abuzz with the news of Vincent's arrest. Many of the young women on campus seemed relieved. My guess was that he had cornered them too, but they were afraid of pressing charges.

Many of the other professors on campus seemed surprised. The guy hid his obsession well. Some of the female professors, however, were not astonished at all. Either way, my classes were more of a study hall as everyone talked about the arrest of a college professor.

I used the time to get ahead on some of my school work. This way I could go to the party with Greg and not have to worry about school, or work. After my time playing detective, I needed a break. I wanted a break.

The only person who could ruin a good time would be—

"Rachel," I said, "you can't expect me to stop living just to satisfy your need for peace."

"But you promised. And think of all the times I got you out of trouble," she pleaded.

"After you got me into trouble," I reminded her.

"Look, I haven't had a chance to go out with Greg in a while. For once, I have a day off from both school and work. I plan on having a little fun."

"So catching my murderer means nothing to you anymore?"

"Rachel," I said, "It's not like that. We know who did it. Professor Vincent was arrested today. Detective Shorts knows that Reiss killed you and covered up the crime. He also knows that Reiss has been stealing from the evidence locker and giving drugs to Vincent. It's only a matter of time until the guy is arrested. After that, he might confess."

"But what if he doesn't?"

"He'll still go to prison," I reminded her. "Look, I know you want him tried for your murder, but without that video evidence it might not happen. At least he'll still go to prison and be off the streets."

"I just wanted him tried for what happened to me," said Rachel. "I want people to know that Tom didn't do it."

"The only way that might happen is if we get a confession. Detective Reiss isn't that stupid."

"You're right," said Rachel. "I guess we did what we could."

"Right," I said. "It's time to let the cops handle it. I am going to have some fun tomorrow and try to be a normal college kid."

I was glad that Rachel relented. What did she expect me to do? I had already solved the case and gave what I had to Detective Shorts. Hopefully, the system would take care of it. All I needed to do was stay away from Detective Reiss.

Jackie waltzed through the door with a couple of bags. Just as I thought; she had gone shopping and bought costumes for the both of us.

"We are all set for tomorrow night," she said. She put the bags down and dumped the contents. "I bought you an Egyptian costume. And for me, I'm going to be a Chinese Empress."

"Considering you're part Chinese, don't you think it's a bit cliché?"

"Not at all. And I'm part Korean, remember? Besides, it was either this or the clown."

"I see your point," I said, picking up my costume. Sometimes I wondered if Jackie was made of money. She worked, but always had a lot of cash. "Where did you get the money for this?"

"I have a rich uncle," replied Jackie.

I didn't know if she was pulling my leg or telling the truth. I figured she had someone who gave her money. "As long as it isn't illegal," I joked.

"Well… you know," smiled Jackie.

The next evening arrived and not soon enough for me. I wasn't the only one stoked for this parade. The entire complex was abuzz with excitement, the same with downtown. Apparently, the parade, and after party, was a big deal.

I twirled in front of a floor length mirror, admiring myself in my costume. Jackie had helped me with my makeup. "Are we meeting Greg there?" I asked her.

They had planned this entire affair as a surprise for me. "Yeah, he'll meet us there," she replied.

"You look good," said Rachel.

"You think so? Thanks." I twirled again.

"You know, in the time I lived here, I never did go to the parade," said Rachel.

"You should come," I invited. "Besides, you could probably get on one of the floats."

Rachel beamed at my suggestion. "I just might do that." She disappeared.

Same old Rachel, I thought. Despite the trouble she caused, I had grown fond of her. She was a good friend despite the fact that she was dead.

Jackie and I left the apartment and went to the parade. We took her car since mine still smelled of onions. She managed to find a parking space right next to the beginning of the parade. I don't know how she did it. Leave it to Jackie to find something. Even if it was the best parking space in town.

Greg met us and led us to where he had already set up camp. "I have food and drinks," he said.

"You guys outdid yourself," I said.

"We figured you needed some time out," said Jackie. "And not at a bar where you try to corner a killer."

I grinned sheepishly. I appreciated what they did, and they were right, I had been a bit reckless lately; and stressed.

The paraded started and all those gathered screamed with excitement. Each float was filled with ghouls, ghosts, and skeletons. Jack o' lanterns littered the sidewalk. I oohed and aahed with the rest of the crowd. People pushed against us as they passed by. With the streets so crowded, it was a wonder anyone could move around.

The next float that rolled by had a giant blown up

ghost on it. Black cats surrounded it along with a mesh of pumpkin lights. I nearly choked when I noticed who was on it. Rachel. She sat atop the blown up ghost. She waved at me with a huge grin. I waved back, pleased that she was having some fun.

Rachel jumped off the ghost, causing it to lean back and forth. People marveled at it, thinking that it was part of the show. I laughed out loud.

"What?" asked Greg.

"Just Rachel," I said. "She caused the ghost to move."

"She's here?"

"Of course she's here," I said. "I invited her." My tone ended the conversation.

Just as the parade got to the halfway point, nature called. I frowned. Why is it you always need a bathroom just when there isn't one around? I excused myself. They offered to come with me, but I turned them down. No point in making a big family trip to the bathroom.

The crowd had worsened as I navigated my way to a bathroom. I weaved as best I could. Mostly, I just shoved people out of my way. Some complained, but I ignored them. Did they honestly expect not to get pushed around a bit in this mess?

Naturally, when I reached the bathroom, a line snaked around to the outside and around the corner of the building. I glanced over at the men's room. No one. And guys wonder why women get crazy when it comes to going to the restroom.

I ran over to the men's room. Cautiously, I opened the door. "Hello?" I called.

No answer.

Thinking it was safe, I went in and locked the door. I did my business really quick. Believe it or not, there was actually soap in the dispenser. I don't think most men bother to wash their hands.

I slowly opened the door and peeked outside. Thinking the coast was clear, I slipped out quickly and ran into a guy trying to get in the bathroom. He glared at me, cocking his head so that his pirate hat almost fell off.

"What?" I said. "Have you seen the line at the women's room?"

I ran off, leaving him to ponder my statement. Now that my bladder felt relieved, I wormed my way back to Jackie and Greg. The place was more packed than it was a minute ago. Talk about a popular event.

Calloused fingers wrapped themselves around my arm. A sudden jerk yanked me off my feet. I struggled to get away. My masked assailant dragged my down an alley and away from the parade.

A hand clamped over my mouth, preventing me from screaming. I bit it. In response, I received a blow to my face. A gag was shoved in my mouth and my arms were pinned behind my back. I squirmed as best I could, but it was useless. The man had a firm hold on me.

He dragged me further down the dark alley until the screams of the crowd faded. I lost my breath as the man forced me against a hard brick wall. The foul gag was ripped from my mouth.

"Go ahead and scream," said the man. "No one will hear you." He removed his mask.

Words can't describe what I thought. Detective Reiss stood before me, bearing down on me. Even the wrath of God could not compare to this man's features. He wrapped his fingers around my throat.

"Let me go," I wailed.

Reiss laughed maniacally.

I thought I saw movement behind him. He noticed my eyes flicker and whipped around. Nothing.

"Hoping someone will save you? No one knows where you are. By the time your friends find you, you will be as talkative as that Rachel."

His foul breath curled my toes. "Why did you do it?" I asked. "Why'd you kill her?"

"You're about to die and all you care about is why I killed some stupid college kid?"

I kept my mouth shut.

"You saw that video. You know what would have happened if she had sent it to the station. I couldn't let it happen. Though maybe I should have killed that Vincent then too, but at the time I needed him. I got him the drugs and he sold them on campus.

"Don't look surprised. Every town and college has a dark side. It was a sweet deal. We both made a lot of money. Vincent's problem is he can't keep his pants zipped. If he had, I wouldn't have had to kill that other girl to keep her silent.

"But then that Rachel had to stumble upon us and tape the whole thing on her phone. I chased after her at first, but she got away. Imagine my surprise when I saw her running across the campus, acting all frightened. I followed her. I managed to catch her before she could send that video, but not before she managed to hide it.

"When the captain put me in charge of the case, I could not have planned it more perfectly. Certain pieces of evidence disappeared. I was disappointed when I couldn't pin it on her boyfriend. Doesn't matter. I got away. Her death remains unsolved. Just like yours."

I kneed him in the groin. He loosened his grip just enough for me to push him away. Unfortunately, my costume was not built for running. Reiss grabbed me and threw me to the ground. Bits of broken glass burned as they dug into my skin. He kicked me in the stomach.

"You are proving to be more trouble than you are worth," said Reiss as he circled me. "I don't know how you found out about Rachel, or that phone, but you know way too much." He rammed his foot into my stomach again. "You are a pain. At least you'll bother me no more."

I heard the crackling of plastic. Reiss unrolled a bunch of plastic as he loomed over me. Before I knew it, he wrapped the plastic tightly around my head, covering my mouth and nose.

I flailed my arms frantically to get him off of me. My lungs burned for air.

"With the madness of the parade, no one will notice you for a long time. They may even think it was a mugging gone bad," bragged Reiss. "Either way, I'll be long gone by the time anyone finds your body."

My world began to go black. My mind refused to focus as lack of oxygen got to me. A loud clang echoed in the alley. Reiss dropped me.

"What the…" he began.

I heard him gasp as something hard rammed into him, causing him to double over. He moved around as some invisible force chased him.

Despite being released, I was unable to free myself from the suffocating plastic. I lay sprawled on the ground, waiting the inevitable. Hands grasped me. They tore at the plastic, ripping it from my mouth.

I sucked in air.

"Mel! Mel!" Both Greg and Jackie bent over me, helping me up. I answered them by breathing deeply.

"How'd you find me?" I asked them.

"That's a long story," said Jackie. "Rachel whispered something about you being in trouble. When you didn't return, I called Detective Shorts."

I glanced over and saw Detective Shorts cuffing Reiss. I felt a phone being shoved into my hand. Looking up, I saw Rachel.

"It's all on here," she said. "Make sure that Shorts guy gets it."

"Miss Summers," said Detective Shorts as he walked up to me, "are you all right? Do you need an ambulance?"

"I'll be fine," I said.

Detective Shorts must have seen the pain in my face and waved a paramedic over. "Mr. Reiss has refused to say anything. Can you tell me what happened?"

I handed Detective Shorts the phone. He took it. "Just press play," I said.

Detective Shorts brought up the video that Rachel had recorded. It had everything: Reiss' confession to stalking me, his intention to kill me, and his confession to murdering Rachel. "This should put him away for a long time. Good thinking; recording everything."

"Mel, you play dangerously."

I turned and saw Tiny.

"We ran into him in our effort to find you," said Greg.

After the paramedic examined me and said I would be fine, my friends led me away. We walked past the parked patrol cars. Everyone stared at the commotion. I guess a bunch of cop cars with flashing lights is more interesting than any parade.

"You bitch," Reiss spat at me. "This isn't over. I'll come for you. You can be sure of that."

Usually, I am an easy going person, but that guy really got under my skin. I had had enough of his garbage. I marched up to him when no one was looking. Using the combined energy of my anger and strength, I seized Reiss by the back of the neck and bashed his face three times into the hood of the car.

"This is for Rachel," I said with each bang. "This is for trying to kill me! And this is for being a complete scumbag!"

I stalked off, pleased with my work.

"I think I'm a bad influence on you," said Rachel. She smacked Reiss in the back of the head.

"Well, you know what they say..." I began. "Sugar and spice—"

"—and not so nice," finished Rachel.

We high fived each other. At that point I didn't care if people thought I was crazy as I slapped thin air.

"Did you see that?" yelled Reiss, "That bitch broke—"

"Did what?" demanded Detective Shorts. "This?" He bashed Reiss' face into the hood of the car. "You know," he said, getting close to Reiss' face, "you're going away for a long time with this confession. You know what they do to cops in prison? Especially dirty cops?" Shorts shoved Reiss toward a uniformed officer. "Get this trash out of here."

After I finished giving my statement to the cops, Detective Shorts released my friends and me. In the car, I got the entire story of how they found me.

"Like I said," said Jackie, "Rachel whispered to me that you were in trouble. Greg and I followed her. That's when we met Tiny."

"They told me you were in trouble," he said, "so, of course I came along."

"That noise in the alley told us where you were," added Greg. "Tiny ripped Reiss right off of you after he seemed to take a hit from some unseen force."

"Thanks guys. Especially you, Rachel," I said.

"I have my moments," said Rachel.

"And we found that guy that broke into your apartment," said Tiny. "Reiss paid him to rough you up a bit and paid someone else to take Greg's car."

"Did you take them to the police?" I asked.

"I'm sure the cops will find them at some point," replied Tiny. "Right now, Sombrero and the boys took them on a nice long ride on a very lonely highway."

When I got home that night, I fell straight into bed, and was out cold.

Chapter 12

Several days passed after my near death incident. Something I'd rather not repeat. I hadn't seen Rachel in all that time. I hoped she had finally moved on.

"You got something from the college," said Jackie handing me a letter.

I ripped it opened, hoping it wasn't a bill, or equally, bad news. Instead, it was a check and a letter. The letter was short and to the point. It stated that since Professor Vincent was involved in illicit activities, and was arrested, all classes that he taught were cancelled for the semester. The check was a refund for taking his course. Add to that the fact that everyone who had registered for his class would receive full credit for it anyway.

I guess the university wished to avoid a lawsuit.

Especially since a flourish of girls came forward and filed harassment charges.

"Wow, a refund from the university. That rarely happens."

I turned around and there stood Rachel. "Rachel," I said, "I thought you'd have moved on by now."

"Close," said Rachel. "I wanted to give you this." She placed a necklace in my palm. It was a silver dolphin. "I want you to have it," she continued. "I don't need it anymore. It's a thank you present."

"Rachel, I can't."

"Take it. You were the first to listen to me. The first to truly care about catching the guy that killed me."

"It's beautiful," I said.

"Dolphins always were my favorite animal."

"So I guess this is good-bye."

"Yeah, it's time I moved on. Call it Heaven or crossing over if you like, but I know where I belong now, and it's time I go where we all do when we die. My grandmother is waiting for me."

"See you around," I said.

"Oh, I'm sure we'll meet again," said Rachel. "Just don't follow me anytime soon."

I chuckled. "You can count on that. Good-bye, Rachel."

She vanished.

"Hey, Mel, what's up?" asked Jackie, reentering the room.

"Nothing," I said.

"Where's Rachel?"

"She left," I replied.

What else could I say? The time had come for her to move forward. The same for me. Life goes on.

Get book 2 in the series:

Frogs, Snails, And A Lot Of Wails

About the Author

Ms. McNulty began writing short stories at an early age. That passion continued through college until she published her first book: Legends Lost: Amborese under the pen name of Nova Rose. Since then, she has gone on to publish a mystery series, children's books, and even a dystopian series.

Recently, her grandmother was diagnosed with Alzheimer's, causing her to visit her grandparents and record her grandfather's memoirs before they become lost. The final result is Grandpa's Stories: The 20th Century as My Grandfather Lived It. She did this to preserve her family history before it becomes lost.

Ms. McNulty currently lives in West Virginia, where she enjoys hiking, being outside, crocheting, or simply sitting around and doing nothing. She continues writing and is busy working on the next book in her Mellow Summers Series.

More by Janet McNulty

The Mellow Summers Series

Sugar And Spice And Not So Nice
Frogs, Snails, And A Lot Of Wails
An Apple A Day Keeps Murder Away
Three Little Ghosts
Oh Holy Ghost
Where Trouble Roams
Two Ghosts Haunt A Grove
Trick Or Treat Or Murder
Roses Are Red...He's Dead
Double, Double, Nothing But Trouble
Ring Around The Rosy, Not ANother Ghosty
Hickory Dickory Dock The Ghost In The Clock
Violets Ate Blue More Trouble Brews

Hey Diddle Diddle The Zombie In The Middle
Easy As Pie Until Someone Dies

Mellow Summers moves to Vermont to attend college, accompanied by her friend Jackie. They soon find themselves running into ghosts and one mystery after another.

The Solaris Saga

Solaris Seethes
Solaris Seeks
Solaris Strays
Solaris Soars

Every myth has a beginning.

After escaping the destruction of her home planet, Lanyr, with the help of the mysterious Solaris, Rynah must put her faith in an ancient legend. Never one to believe in stories and legends, she is forced to follow the ancient tales of her people: tales that also seem to predict her current situation.

Forced to unite with four unlikely heroes from an unknown planet (the philosopher, the warrior, the lover, the inventor) in order to save the Lanyran people, Rynah and Solaris embark on an adventure that will shatter everything Rynah once believed.

The Enchained Trilogy

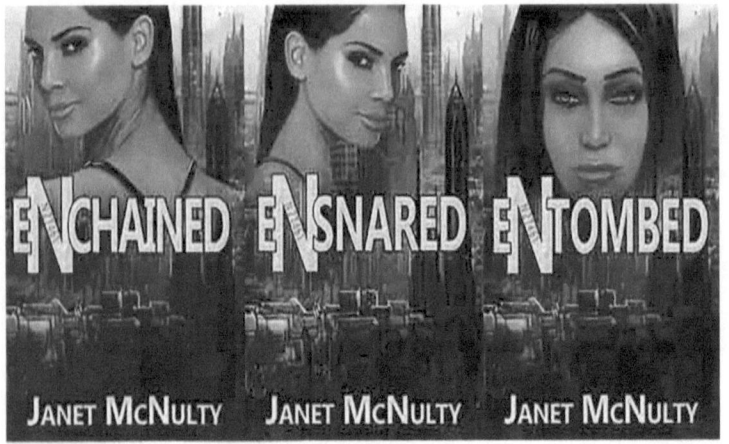

Enchained
Ensnared
Entombed

**Weakness is failure.
Failure is death.**

Having spent her entire life secluded in the Martial Diplomatic Corps, Noni passes the final test, achieving the coveted position as arbiter of Arel. Placed under the tutelage of a seasoned veteran, Noni will see her city for the first time and learn that not everything is as she had been taught to believe.

The Dystopia Trilogy

Dystopia
Tempered Steel
Liberty's Torch

**Imagine living in a world where
everything you do is controlled.**

Dana Ginary lives in a world where every aspect of her life is controlled by the Dystopian Government. Forced to work in Waste Management, her life becomes a nightmare with hunger and survival is her only constant. Before she knows it, she is caught up in a resistance movement and exiled from Dystopia, forced to find her way in the barren wastelands. While there, she must learn to live independently and discover how far she is willing to go to live and achieve freedom.

The Legends Lost Series

Published under Nova Rose

Tesnayr
Amborese
Galdin

Enter the Lands of Tesnayr and join on an epic fantasy adventure that spans over 1,500 years.

Begin with Tesnayr, the first king of the five lands as he unites the against a savage foe bent on their destruction.

Next, Join Amborese as she fights reclaim the throne after her family was forced to flee from it.

Thinking peace has finally entered the land, follow Galdin as he returns to Tesnayr to find it greatly hanged. Barbarians, led by a mysterious sorcerer, burn and destroy as they go. And only Galdin can stop them if he chooses to accept his fate.

Visit www.legendslosttrilogy.com to learn more about the Legends Lost Trilogy.

Grandpa's Stories

My grandfather grew up in Arizona during the 1920s and 1930s. One week after the attack on Pearl Harbor he joined the Navy. During the summer of 2012, my mother visited him and recorded his stories about growing up, World War II, and his time as an employee at the Pacific Bell Telephone Company. This is the history of the 20th century as he lived it. These recordings make up this book. These are his words.

www.ingramcontent.com/pod-product-compliance
Lightning Source LLC
Chambersburg PA
CBHW020655180626
46816CB00003B/1296